*With sincere appreciation for all you do.*
*Jake.*

When the wrong note goes to the wrong girl,
Jake Flynn finds out he has a lot to learn...about
women!

Dear Reader,

Well, summer may be drawing to a close but don't worry, this month's selection from Desire™ is as sizzling hot as ever! There's lots of fun to be had too with mistaken identities, mix-ups and even a matchmaking comet to contend with!

Firstly, **Man of the Month**, Shane Nichols, gets himself in a muddle in Anne McAllister's *The Cowboy Steals a Lady*. He kidnaps his best friend's girl in order to stop her marrying another man—only he steals the wrong woman! And what a mix-up in Leandra Logan's *The Education of Jake Flynn*! Jake sends two very different presents to two sisters. But he's in for a surprise when the 'sensible' sister ends up with the sexy present.

Now to that comet: Elizabeth Bevarly starts her **Comet Fever** trilogy this month with *Bride of the Bad Boy*. Angie Ellison tries to blame a matchmaking comet for her attraction to the mysterious Ethan Zorn. Well, how *else* can she explain her shotgun wedding? Mattie Ryan, on the other hand, knows all the reasons for her marriage of convenience in Sara Orwig's *Her Torrid Temporary Marriage*. But what she can't explain is how things got quite so steamy!

Finally, Metsy Hingle kicks off her **Right Bride, Wrong Groom** series this month with *The Kidnapped Bride*. And in Carole Buck's *Three-Alarm Love* the question is whether this on-off couple will *ever* make it down the aisle!

Happy Reading

The Editors

# The Education of Jake Flynn

## LEANDRA LOGAN

™ SILHOUETTE

*Desire*®

*Silhouette, Silhouette Desire and Colophon
are registered trademarks of Harlequin Books S.A.,
used under licence.*

*First published in Great Britain 1998
Silhouette Books, Eton House, 18-24 Paradise Road,
Richmond, Surrey TW9 1SR*

© Mary Schultz 1996

ISBN 0 373 52027 1

22-9809

*Printed and bound in Spain
by Litografía Rosés S.A., Barcelona*

# LEANDRA LOGAN

Many of you have expressed interest in how I come up with my storylines. Sometimes the answer is simple—and, alas, boring! But in the case of *The Education of Jake Flynn*, provocative images of sultry nights, small-town secrets and outrageous sibling rivalry provided my first sparks of inspiration. I couldn't jot down details fast enough!

With a short and sexy tale in mind, Nadine Jordan sprang to life. The town's pretty young schoolteacher, put on a pedestal, every little boy's first crush. Except she's harbouring a crush of her own for neighbour Jake Flynn, secretly yearning for his return.

Enter Jake Flynn—sexy, vulnerable and streetwise, ready to battle old enemies for his rightful place. Like everyone else, he, too, is foolish enough to envision Nadine on that pedestal. Oh, does he have a lot to learn...

# 1

"So teacher's pet is the teacher now."

The drawled taunt was gentle, teasing and tantalizingly masculine. And music to Nadine Jordan's ears. The eraser in the young schoolteacher's hand stalled on the blackboard as her heart squeezed with joy. Even with her back to the quiet, hollow classroom, she knew for sure: Jake Flynn was truly home again. Right where he belonged.

The news of his impending return had spread like wildfire through the tiny town of Cherry Creek, Georgia, two days ago. She'd been aflame with anticipation ever since, certain that a visit to the grammar school was bound to be at the top of his list.

She carefully set her eraser in the chalk tray at her waist, taking a deep steadying breath. This was it. She was about to make contact with the one man she never could quite shake loose from her memory. But there were uncertainties to temper her enthusiasm. Would he be ready to acknowledge her as a grown woman, more than Charmaine's little sister? Would he see her as a desirable woman? She was determined to have some fun finding out!

She whirled around with bubbling laughter, her strawberry-blond mane taking flight around her shoulders, the hem of her rosebud print dress rising from her knees. "Welcome home, neighbor."

The tall, lean man slouched against the scarred door-jamb straightened and eased into the back of the room. His body was corded strength beneath his snug faded jeans and red plaid shirt. As his face came into clear focus, Nadine couldn't help but note a new leanness to his features, lines fanning his gray eyes, a hardness to his mouth despite his grin.

And why not? His life hadn't been easy. He'd spirited away the town beauty queen, married her, buried her and become a father in between—a lot of living and some hard knocks for someone so young.... Quick tabulation against her own age of twenty-three put him at twenty seven.

He was back home to set things straight. With little more than his pride, it appeared. His clothes were clean, but worn. His black hair was trimmed close with a cut so new that it didn't quite match the tan line at his neck.

"That's no kind of welcome after nine years!" he complained mockingly. He advanced down a side aisle between the rows of neatly aligned desks, dwarfing them with his size.

Nadine's golden lashes fluttered to her flushing cheeks as the old wooden floor creaked beneath his boots. Her second graders—long gone for the weekend—didn't have the weight to make those creaks, or the power to render her totally helpless in this controlled classroom setting. She suddenly found herself in a tussle with her past and present—floating somewhere between the child he knew from yesterday and the woman she was today. Eager and a little frightened, she took bold steps forward.

"Still ownin' every room you enter, I reckon," she lilted, her green eyes twinkling.

He shook his head, holding her gaze with a flicker of admiration. "I have the feeling this is your special place, Nadine."

She beamed appreciatively. "You're right about that, I guess."

He rubbed a finger along his jawline, his gaze growing keen. "Imagine, the little Jordan sister a figure of authority. I'm not sure I'm ready to accept you without those braces and braids."

She balked in protest. "I've changed a lot!"

"You still climb trees?" he wondered hopefully. "I'd feel right at home to know you could still do that."

She glared at him, and was surprised when he instantly exploded with laughter. He was purposely goading her! "Damn you!" she exclaimed, shaking a small fist at him.

Jake's expression grew tender as he moved in closer. "C'mere, honey. Give me a real welcome home." He eagerly gathered the petite Nadine into his arms, releasing a groan of pleasure as she snuggled up against him. She was the sweet Southern springtime of his dreams, from her loose floral dress, to her faint honeysuckle cologne, to her flowing, shimmery hair.

Home. He'd been in his small hometown for half a day, in the school for half an hour, and it wasn't until this moment that he felt truly settled. Nadine evoked comfort, trust and joy, the cozy security of yesterday. The Flynns and the Jordans were lifelong next-door neighbors by luck, extended family by choice.

He released her reluctantly, with an appreciative look. "Let me take a good long look at you."

"You already did," she sassed back brightly.

His grin broadened with traces of naughty intent. "So I did."

Nadine swayed back toward her desk with demure afterthought, remembering where they were and who she was. She had a sterling image to uphold in the school and she'd never once betrayed that image. Ironic as it seemed, it was that steady, sedate persona that had probably drawn Jake to her now, most likely before he'd even unpacked his bags. She didn't mind. She wanted to be everything to him. First the teacher he was bound to need for his daughter, then eventually the lover he'd most surely come to desire for himself.

"I suppose Dad told you how things are," he ventured to guess, sidling up to the front of her ancient wooden desk. His eyes fell to the flat polished surface between them. Her papers, pencils and books were in order, suggesting primness, neatness.

It was bound to be a direct reflection of the mature, focused woman Nadine had become. And exactly what he'd hoped for.

"Will did fill us in." She nodded, sinking into her heavy varnished chair. "Figured you'd want us to know, being like family."

"Yes, of course," he assured her with new urgency.

"You do plan to stay on, don't you?" Nadine couldn't resist asking. "I mean, after this battle with your in-laws is over?"

"That's exactly my plan. I hope you'll be able to find it in your heart to help us. I know I teased you a bit when you were young—"

Her emerald eyes flashed. "You and Charmaine tortured me relentlessly, Jake Flynn!"

He chuckled guiltily. "You were always full of compassion, honey. Even when you were just a tee-toncy girl.'' He picked up a ceramic apple from the nicked wooden desktop and measured it in his huge roughened hands.

Nadine watched the play of his fingers, a sensuous longing warming her insides. There was nothing tiny about her now. She was fully grown, with fully blossomed appetites. She was determined that he come to understand that.

It was with great effort that she mentally shifted to the mission that had brought him over to Lincoln Grammar School in the first place.

''I was sorry to learn about Rosemary's death,'' she offered quietly, her eyes never leaving his hands. ''Lung cancer in such a young woman can't be all that common.''

''It was a sorry thing,'' he agreed quietly. ''We were quite happy in our own way. Would've been married a whole nine years this summer.''

''I'm sure she was quite content as your wife,'' Nadine speculated softly.

''As content as a woman can be with her family against her,'' Jake returned grimly. ''Those damn Parnells, driving us out of town with their pressure for the abortion. Rosemary could've used her mama's support back then. Really missed Thelma in the end. I was preparing to bring her back from Cleveland, but she didn't last.'' He shook his dark head in sorrow. ''That was fourteen months ago.''

''Will said you lost your construction company along the way.''

''It just slipped through my fingers as I tried to keep our family together,'' he affirmed on a sigh. ''I've been working for someone else almost round the clock since then, trying to pay off Rosemary's hospital bills. Finally,

finally, I was beginning to see an end to the struggle and was looking forward to spending quality time with my daughter, Amy Jo. Then the letter came…''

''The letter from Rosemary's parents' attorney,'' Nadine guessed.

''Yes! Calder and Thelma Parnell hired some high-falutin' Savannah lawyer named Milton Soames to probe into my business, and assert their right to bring up Amy Jo.'' He dipped his head lower, his expression growing thunderous. ''First those hypocrites tried to terminate my baby in their daughter's womb, and now that she's grown up precious, they want to draw her into the Parnell fold.''

''Milton Soames has a reputation for being sharp,'' she told him bluntly. ''Charmaine works for Len Tyler now, you know, as his secretary. Len's still the only lawyer in Cherry Creek and has his finger on the pulse of every legal skirmish within the town limits.'' Nadine winced as his face lit up at the mention of her big sister's name, but she kept her tone even. ''Charmaine says the Parnells approached Len Tyler first about building a case against you as an unfit parent. Len found the idea revolting, so Calder Parnell sought help at the Savannah law firm.''

''After failing to make Rosemary happy, you'd think they'd hang back in shame! But oh, no, they see something they want and they make a wild grab!'' Jake swallowed back a sour taste as he dwelled on the Parnells. The letter he'd received from them through the attorney had outlined all the advantages that they could provide Amy Jo, the same ones Rosemary'd had growing up. How sadly ironic that Rosemary had been miserable as a girl, despite the Parnell wealth. Calder had been forever busy with his blasted peanut farm, and Thelma had been no better with her committees and charities. Lonely, needy Rosemary, the town's only society girl, had chosen him, of all people, to fall for. Popular football hero Jake Flynn—average grades, average ambition, above average charm.

Jake and his father Will were not the sort of in-laws the Parnells had in mind. Plans to separate them by sending Rosemary off to college in Atlanta were swiftly formed on the eve of high school graduation. Then the Parnells' world shattered when Rosemary became pregnant. More plans were made, this time to terminate the new life inside her. Seeing no other option, the eighteen-year-olds ran off to get married, have their child and start a brand-new life together.

Cherry Creek would've been a permanent part of Jake's past if Rosemary hadn't gotten sick. But she had, and uncontrollable circumstances had left him in a helpless spin. A spin that had led back home.

Nadine felt a rush of compassion as she watched Jake's features twist in turmoil. But it was her nature to look at all sides of an issue, so she had thoroughly examined the Parnells' motivations, as well. Despite their vain ways, Rosemary's defection had to have left a huge empty space in their hearts. It was obviously a void they hoped to fill with their granddaughter. It was a shame they were going about it in such a clumsy, negative way.

"Everything will be all right, Jake," Nadine said, breaking the thoughtful silence between them. "Despite this problem, Cherry Creek is still a wonderful place to raise a child."

Jake's features brightened under her encouraging look. Lord, she'd grown lovely. She'd been a cute teenager, but she was a woman now, mature and capable. He reached across the desk suddenly and seized her soft slender hands in his. ''More than anything in the world I want to shake off that powerless feeling I've been living under lately, honey,'' he confided in a fervent rush. ''I want to control my destiny again. Start a small home-improvement business here. Give Amy Jo the foundation she deserves.''

''Of course, Jake,'' Nadine breathed, her heart hammering. Certainly that plan had to include a new wife, didn't it? How encouraging that he was already sharing his goals with her! She struggled to keep a calm front. ''This is your home just as much as it is the Parnells'. You just have to stake your claim!''

His raven brows narrowed over glittery gray eyes. ''Yes. Setting things straight with them will be the first order of business.''

''And the rest will fall into place,'' she chirped.

Jake kept her hands in his for a long revitalizing moment, until they heard footsteps outside the doorway. They broke contact as the principal, Mildred Brooks, appeared with a youngster the size of Nadine's eight-year-old students.

Nadine's eyes widened in amazement. Could this be Amy Jo Flynn? It was hard to believe the glamorous Rosemary had given birth to this small ragamuffin lost in a baggy flannel top and denim bottoms and a boyish cap. It was a hot and steamy day in April and the girl was dressed for the dead of winter, covered from head to toe. It had to be a protective shell.

The second Amy Jo caught sight of Jake, she tore away from the tall, reedy woman in the drab gray suit and bolted to his side with her green shirttail flying.

''I've given her the tour,'' Miss Brooks announced, openly taken aback by the child's abruptness. She was

a formal educator from the old school who expected awe
and complacency from her students.

Nadine smiled at her superior, determined to lighten
the moment. "So Amy Jo will be joining my class for
certain then?"

"Yes, she will," Miss Brooks affirmed with an exasperated look. "It was nice to meet you, young lady.
Nice to see you again, Jake." With a curt nod, she dis-
appeared from view, her heels echoing hollowly down
the hallway.

Jake rolled his eyes. "I hated to leave you with her,
Amy Jo. But she insisted."

Amy Jo, nervously twisting her small hands together,
favored him with a scowl from beneath the bill of her
blue baseball cap.

Nadine rounded the desk and sat on the front edge so
she was more level with her new student. As she
smoothed the folds of her full cotton skirt, she couldn't
help noticing that the child's fingernails were chewed to
the quick. "I'm Miss Jordan," she said in introduction,
"here in school, that is. Back at home you can just call
me Nadine, like everybody else does."

"I told Amy Jo all about you," Jake murmured, graz-
ing his daughter's cheek with his finger. "How you and
Charmaine live next door to Grandpa Will. How you
teach the second grade."

"That old lady tried to take my hat off," Amy Jo
croaked in indignation.

Nadine found herself tempted to do the same thing.
There was a tangled nest of black hair under it, in need
of some tender loving care. As a matter of fact, it appeared that she could use a good polish from head to
toe. Nadine swallowed back her exasperation. *Oh, Jake,
how could you let this girl's appearance go? Rosemary*

*must be spittin' tacks up in the heavens.* Thankfully, the other children were long home, missing the opportunity to poke fun at this oddly dressed, discontented child. Luckily, it was a Friday, which gave them the weekend for repairs. And then there was her academic level to consider. Chances were, she was behind in her studies. And it was so close to the end of the school year. Would Amy Jo be capable of completing the courses expected of her, so she could move up a grade next fall?

Objectively speaking, this first impression of Amy Jo wasn't especially favorable. Sulky and set apart, Mildred Brooks might tell the Parnells. Ammunition against Jake already!

"I don't like that principal, Daddy," Amy Jo declared fervently, folding her spindly arms across her chest.

"Miss Brooks can be a little stern, but she's fair," Nadine soothed, forcing confidence into her tone.

Amy Jo flashed her a wary look, then addressed Jake. "Can we go back to Grandpa's house now?"

"Let's all go home," Nadine suggested brightly. "I'll just get my sweater and purse."

As they descended the school's wooden steps to the street, Jake tried to give Amy a sense of the place, explaining that the old white clapboard school had once been set apart from the residential area, but after World War II homes had gradually been built up to its property lines. Amy Jo was full of questions, anxious to compare it to Cleveland.

Nadine approved of the girl's curiosity, quickly convinced that Amy Jo was a bright little star beneath her layers of cotton, just aching to shine if given the chance.

The walk back to their respective homes on Simpson Street was three-quarters of a mile, to the oldest section of town. They strolled along the wide cracked sidewalks beneath the sun-dappled trees. Nadine positioned herself so that Amy Jo was between them and the most favored in conversation. Jake encouraged his daughter to talk about the room that Grandpa Will had prepared for her upstairs, with pale blue chiffon curtains and a handmade quilt bedspread. Nadine admitted to helping Will with the decorating. For the first time, Amy Jo offered her a genuine smile.

"This street still is the prettiest sight in the world," Jake remarked when they finally turned off Chestnut onto Simpson. "Especially on a spring day like today."

"Yes, I suppose it could be," Nadine agreed, nonplussed. She walked its length so frequently that she had lost sight of its charm. She took for granted the fact that all of the grand old homes were kept up nicely, with neatly clipped green lawns and flower boxes adorning shiny windows. The street itself was nearly a century old, and sometime during the early years the city planners had planted red maples along the boulevards. Today, in the middle of springtime, their branches created an awning over the street and walks, a cover of blossoming red leaves.

Their heels hitting the pebbly squares of concrete was the only sound between them for awhile. They eventually reached the end of the street, where the Jordans' gray gabled two-story with red shutters sat beside the Flynns' plainer white saltbox. Black ornamental fencing enclosed the Jordans' front yard, so Nadine paused at the gate to say goodbye.

Jake, to her delight, didn't seem in any hurry to move on as he scanned their properties. "So your parents moved away," he commented.

"Yes, to Arizona," she explained, fingering the steel gate latch. "Mom wanted to live near her sister in Phoenix. I, for one, can't imagine living anywhere but right here.''

He nodded. ''I can understand that. Leaving this street, my house, my folks, was the toughest thing I've ever done.''

''Coming back has to be the bravest thing you've ever done,'' Nadine replied tenderly, her full lips curving.

His eyes crinkled in the sunshine. ''You still have a way of making me feel older, wiser, and very capable. I appreciate it.''

''I don't have to be a gangly girl to look up to you, Jake,'' Nadine pointed out, laughing when he gently cuffed her chin. It was the same sort of intimacy they used to share, with a new sensual awareness tossed in. Nadine wished she could bottle the feeling like a love potion and splash it all over them every day, forever more.

''Why, Jake Flynn! Is that you? It is you!''

So much for pat love spells and easy conquests, Nadine griped inwardly as her sister called out from behind their front screen door. Charmaine wasted no time sashaying across the porch and down the walk. Her lovely face was alight with surprise—as if Charmaine wasn't expecting him! As if the whole setup—her being home early from the law office, dressed in a tight yellow knit dress pulled off the shoulders—wasn't openly contrived. No matter, the show was extremely effective.

''Hey, Sassy.'' Jake laughed as Charmaine burst through the front gate and leapt into his arms. He swung her off her bare feet. And she kissed him full on the mouth.

Nadine frowned. No time for shoes, but the makeup was artful.

Just once, couldn't she be referred to as the sassy one?

Nadine set her hands on her hips, biting back envy over Charmaine's position and annoyance over her nerve. Of course Charmaine would feel comfortable kissing him this way, for she was in Jake's class back in school, had even dated him before Rosemary had caught his eye. Rosemary had been the only rival Charmaine had ever considered a serious threat. Since her departure, Charmaine had easily slipped into the spot of town beauty, habitually taking whatever she pleased whenever it pleased her. And she did it so charmingly, nobody seemed to mind much.

A tiny inner voice of reason cautioned Nadine that it would be far wiser to continue concealing her interest in Jake, rather than risk enhancing his desirability in Charmaine's eyes. Charmaine was bound to be all the more intrigued with him if she knew that Nadine wanted him so badly.

Nadine held no grudge against her more flamboyant sister. They were friendly rivals at worst. But this time the stakes were higher. They weren't vying for the same lipstick, or lingerie, or television remote.

For the first time ever, they would be sparring for a real live man!

Ultimately it was the third female on the scene that seized the spotlight. Amy Jo grew weary of the couple's embrace and wedged in between them. Charmaine, forced to acknowledge the child's existence, did so with a startled cry of complaint. She took a full step back and sized up the situation with her keen instinct. "It's all right, sugar," she eventually cooed in comforting counterpoint. "Your daddy and I used to date a long time ago. Went through school together, too, starting over at Lincoln."

"Jake and Amy Jo were just over to the school for a

visit,'' Nadine told her sister. "We had a real nice time.''

"Caught her clappin' erasers, I suppose,'' Charmaine teased with a smile. "Used to be a punishment back when we were in school, Amy Jo. Nadine liked it so much she'd misbehave on purpose just for the chance. Became a teacher for the same reason.''

Nadine gasped in surprise as Amy Jo brightened noticeably under Charmaine's brilliant smile.

"Charmaine stood in the corner so many times back then that she finally grew cross-eyed,'' Nadine gibed in return, pleased to get a giggle from the child.

Jake watched as Nadine and Charmaine exchanged the catlike smirk considered the sister's trademark, their small lush mouths curved with coy confidence, eyes gleaming with desirous promise. Even now, in their mid-twenties, they could still pass for twins, despite the four years between them. Close scrutiny did prove that Nadine's mass of blond hair held a tinge of red, and Charmaine's green eyes were flecked with gold. Those were the only physical differences that set them apart.

Their temperaments were more sharply defined, however.

Nadine, quiet, reliable and even tempered, fit the mold of the small-town schoolteacher.

Charmaine was the town temptress, with artistically applied makeup and bangles down to her ankles.

With any luck, both would play an important role in his future.

Nadine would see him through his days.

Charmaine would see him through his nights.

If things worked out, he'd garner the best of both of them, never needing a wife again!

# 2

"**W**hat do you mean you plan to never marry again!" Will Flynn exploded over his son's declaration an hour later as they stood in the Flynn kitchen.

Jake reached over the open refrigerator door to clamp a hand over Will's mouth. "Keep your voice down, Dad. Amy Jo might hear you."

"All right!" Will relented as he peeled Jake's fingers from his copper-colored face. "But would you please explain this lunacy to me."

Jake removed a carton of milk and whisked the fridge door shut again. "I—" He broke off, staring at the faded fruit-figured wallpaper covering the walls of the cheery country-flavored room. The paper was fifteen years old, at least, and brought him an odd sense of nostalgic comfort. This place was just the safe haven he and Amy Jo needed. More than anything he wanted to drift back to a simpler time, a less stressful way of life. Jake felt that in the course of a decade he'd seen everything and done everything; that he'd come full circle. He'd built up a business, produced a child, lost a wife. He felt as old as dirt and as spent as last month's salary. The last thing on his mind was starting over at the courtship stage with somebody else. Rosemary had been his everything. They'd weathered their final growth spurt together, then eased into adulthood with a few emotional battle scars and a more mature outlook. Their youth and detachment from family could have led to disaster, but instead it strengthened their puppy love, evolved into a oneness enjoyed by only the best marriages.

Will was waiting for an explanation, his eyes keen, his leathery face as wrinkled as a peach pit. But Jake had never been a big talker. He wasn't prepared to pour out his heart to his father. Despite the fact that they'd always had a good relationship, it would take time to adjust to each other all over again.

But Jake could see the fury burning in Will's eyes. His granddaughter didn't have a mama, and he wanted answers!

"I can't see going through it all again," he finally blurted out. "It's risky and unbearably painful. I figure Amy Jo and I are better off sticking together as a pair."

"You're too young to feel this way!"

"Rosemary was young, too," Jake returned soberly, setting the carton on the table with thump.

Will grunted in disapproval, then to Jake's amazement, an odd light danced in his eyes. "Your needs will soon eat deeper than your fears," he predicted with confidence. "You'll begin to ache so bad for all the comforts Rosemary gave that you'll be weepin' in your bed at night. And right down the hall will be my precious grandchild, her face in her pillow, weepin' along with ya, wishin' and hopin' for a new mama."

"I can still have it all," Jake assured him with a dismissive wave. "Support, companionship, affection. You'll see."

Will was aghast. "You expect some woman to supply all that with no promises?"

Jake's mouth curved with a trace of sheepishness. "I

figured on dividing up the duties between the two prettiest girls in town.''

Will's bushy white brows jumped. "Charmaine and Nadine. All for you and yours?"

"It's not like I want to own them, Dad. I just want to share like we used to. No false promises to anybody. Just mutual understanding of how things are. Sounds reasonable, doesn't it?"

Will's weathered face sharpened shrewdly. "A little maternal kindness for the girl, a little sultry play for you, eh?"

"Well…" Jake trailed off, acknowledgment in his tone. "They're over the age of consent by a measure. They can say no." He raised a finger of caution as Will opened his mouth. "Don't go all protective on me, Dad."

Will cracked a cagey smile. "I have no intention of protecting you."

"I mean playing the surrogate father to them and you know it!"

"I don't feel like their father," Will swiftly corrected. "Haven't for quite some years."

Jake's gray eyes narrowed. "Our families were blended in the old days. Neighbor helping neighbor."

"Those girls stopped needing an extra daddy a long time ago," Will insisted adamantly.

"And you accepted that?" Jake hooted in disbelief.

"They convinced me."

"Send you a note, a telegram? What?"

"Sent me the kind of a message only they would," his father replied, shuffling over to the window facing the backyard. He pulled back the pumpkin-colored curtains spanning the lower half of the glass. "C'mere."

Jake tromped across the linoleum, his thumbs hooked

in his belt loops. He gazed at the deep property over his father's shoulder. He saw nothing unusual. Just the huge walnut and pecan trees, and the old white gazebo.

"Those girls are mighty smart," Will murmured. "A couple years back, around the time that Rosemary got sick, after their folks moved to the desert, they started coming over. Out there."

Jake peered out the glass in bewilderment. He'd noticed earlier that the old white slatted structure was completely redone, better than new, with an expensive green roof and sturdy, freshly painted planks. "They helped you fix up the gazebo?" he finally guessed.

"Nooo, you stupid fool!" Will heaved his thin chest, summoning the right words for a fresh beginning. "It was tough when your mother died in '88. I was witherin' away back then. And you had your devastating troubles, and I couldn't help you fix things like I used to when you were a boy."

Jake frowned, mentally moving back to that sad time. Hearing that his mother was dying, he, Rosemary and their toddler daughter had arrived in the middle of the night for a covert visit to say goodbye to Jolene. To this day, no one knew they'd ever been back to the house, not even the Jordans. Rosemary had been adamant about keeping the secret then, for all the emotional wounds her parents had inflicted were still so fresh. And she truly felt that her folks didn't deserve to know Amy Jo, their precious princess, full of wonder and delight. "You seemed to rebound after Mom's death," he finally blurted out in surprise.

"I did, up to a point," Will assured him. "Guess I just fell into an unexpected trap of hopelessness. I got to contemplating moving on."

Jake took the full impact of the message with a thudding heart. "I can't believe it, Dad. You wanted to die?"

Will shrugged beneath his blue cotton work shirt. "Happens. Long over it now, of course."

"So what did the sisters do for you?"

"Made me feel like a rip-doodlin' young feller again, that's what!" He turned his profile to Jake and dropped his voice to a rasp, grinning over a mental image. "Started doin' a *fais-dodo* out there in the moonlit shadows, late in the night."

"They did?" Jake swallowed hard. The *fais-dodo* was part of Will's Cajun heritage, an evening party full of provocative dancing. He and the sisters had spent many spellbound hours listening to Will's stories of growing up as a half-breed youth in the Louisiana bayou. Apparently the stories stuck.

Will, measuring his son's face for shock value, was satisfied with his dazed state. "Guess they saw the light on here in the kitchen night after night, noticed that I stopped picking up my paper, going into town."

Jake favored him with a dubious frown. "If you needed cheering, why didn't they bring a coffee cake to the back door?"

"They tried to reach me with food—beaten biscuits, cheese grits, fried chicken, all my favorites. But they knew I wasn't eating 'em."

"So…" Jake prompted.

"So they made up a batch of Thunderbolt punch and left that on my doorstep. An hour later I heard laughter wafting through my screens and caught a glimpse of the most beautiful sight on this earth—two lovely nymphs flitting round among the trees in scanty, floaty fabrics." Will closed his eyes with a grand smile. "Saved my life. I slipped back to my boyhood and worked up my strength remembering all the good things that have ever happened to me. They brought more food and I ate it! Danced on in the night and I watched.''

Jake absorbed the scene his father painted with a measure of incredulity. ''What did you eventually say to each other?''

''Words weren't necessary. They knew I was better when I showed up outside in the midday sun, set on repairing the dilapidated gazebo with my own two hands.'' Will's look was patronizing as he moved away from the windowsill. ''Couldn't have them falling through the rotted flooring, could I?''

Jake's strong jaw slacked with amazement. ''You never spoke of what happened?''

''Some things are just understood between friends.''

Jake was on his father's heels as he moved toward the stove to stir his simmering pot of stew. ''You have that kind of connection with them? Why, I'm not sure even you and I have that depth of understanding.''

''I'm sure we don't at this time,'' Will agreed, dipping his gray head to smell the beefy concoction with appreciation. ''But we'll catch up. This man-to-man talk is a good beginning. The moral of this story is that the Jordan sisters are adult women in every sense of the word, holding down responsible jobs in town, paying taxes, doing all the things grown-ups do.''

Jake made a blustery sound. ''That's obvious!''

''They're no longer the young girls you knew,'' his father added gruffly.

''I gladly concede that they're adults,'' Jake said grandly, folding his arms across his expansive chest.

''With womanly needs the both of them! You still don't seem to fathom that it's far more complicated than it was in the old days! You've returned here with preconceived notions concerning them—sassy Charmaine and sensible Nadine.''

''Right! And I've found it still holds true!''

''Maybe you weren't hearin' me boy,'' the older man said with strained patience. ''It wasn't a case of Nadine cooking up the food and Charmaine dancing round in flimsy scarves. They were in it together. Virtually interchangeable out there in the moonlight.''

Jake raked a hand through his raven hair, avoiding contact with his father's alert eyes. Will had to be wrong about that point. Sure, the sisters resembled each other, but they had distinctly different personalities, each offering something the other could not provide. ''As I see it, Dad, Amy Jo is the female I'm dedicated to right now,'' he hedged.

''I know exactly what you're up to,'' Will said craftily. ''And I'd lecture you for an hour if I thought it was worth it.'' He edged past Jake to the swinging maple door, and leaned on it to peek through to the dimly lit living room. ''Supper's on, Amy Jo,'' he called out cheerily. ''You can leave the television on.''

Jake took three large, shallow bowls from the cupboard and brought them to the stove. ''Let me thank you in advance for butting out.''

''Let me tell you in advance that I don't have to lift a finger to teach you a lesson,'' Will returned with a deep chuckle. ''Somehow, I imagine all that will be taken care of neat and proper.''

''Hold up, Charmaine!'' Nadine called out later that night.

''Why, Nadine,'' Charmaine cried, peering into the Jordans' second-level study, ''you scared the life out of me!'' She clutched the neck of her knee-length chenille robe with long ivory fingers and frowned at her sister. "I thought for certain that you came up here to go straight to bed."

Nadine smiled tolerantly behind the old rolltop desk that served as her homework headquarters. Charmaine was obviously up to something. Her hair, freshly washed and dried, hung like soft golden tinsel around her heaving chest. And her hazel eyes were huge and distracted. "I'm preparing some tests for Amy Jo," Nadine explained evenly.

"Putting her right to work?" Charmaine inquired, waltzing into the cozy brown-and-beige room full of odd pieces of tapestry-covered furniture and framed family photographs. "Wonder if that child would do better with a little fun and glamour in her life."

Nadine shook her honey-red head as she eased a sheet of simple arithmetic problems into a file folder. "It's crucial to guide her into the second-grade mainstream as quickly as possible. Judge Trimble called me this evening, the moment he heard that I am to be Amy Jo's teacher. He's relying on me to measure her aptitude for the custody hearing, sees me as an objective third party in the dispute."

"Well, I guess that's good luck, 'cause it gives Jake an advantage over the Parnells," Charmaine said.

"Of course it does!" Nadine happily agreed. "If Calder and Thelma can't find just cause for the judge to take Amy Jo away from Jake, it isn't going to happen. I'm going to work my head off to throw him in a capable light," she added with a vigorous nod.

"Good plan, I suppose," Charmaine conceded, self-consciously tugging at the lavender cover-up cloaking her slender frame. "Still, I think there's more to a girl's education than the ABCs and the one-two-threes."

"It's a case of priorities," Nadine maintained. "I suspect she's missed her share of school and it's important she catch up. Everything social should fall in behind getting her on track in class. I want to bring good test results to the judge."

Charmaine rolled her expressive eyes. "You'll no doubt see to it."

"Thank you." Nadine smirked as points of pastel chiffon peeped out from beneath her sister's robe. "So, were you on your way out?"

Charmaine's lashes fluttered. "When, Nadine?"

"When I stopped you in the hallway just now," Nadine clarified patiently with a tap of her pencil.

Charmaine reared back, her mouth an open circle of amazement. "At ten-thirty at night? In my robe? Why, never!"

"Well, that's good, because I think it's too late to go calling at the Flynns'."

"You think so?" Charmaine huffed with new candor. She moved to the side window facing the Flynns' and jerked up the fringed shade to peer over at the white saltbox. "Guess it does look dark...." she relented.

Nadine bit back a burst of laughter. Charmaine was so childlike when she was trying to pull a fast one. It was plain to see that she'd planned to skip over to the Flynns' backyard and give Jake a real welcome, in the form of seductive dance. But Nadine was determined to keep her sense of humor, rather than risk appearing envious and territorial. Charmaine's instincts concerning the heart were sharp. "I called Jake to set up some early-morning testing for tomorrow," she explained. "He said Will was already sleeping."

"Will?" Charmaine repeated distractedly.

"Well, yes," Nadine answered guilelessly. "Isn't he

the one you were planning to entertain in your costume? I mean, the well-traveled, more sophisticated Jake has probably seen wilder things on big-city streets at noon hour.''

''You really think so?'' Charmaine queried in a squeak.

Nadine nodded sagely, remembering that all was fair in love and war.

''I suppose I did figure Will might need some cheering up,'' Charmaine faltered in an effort to save face.

''Will's in fine shape,'' Nadine assured her, playing along. ''He has his only son back under his roof, with a granddaughter in the bargain. It's been years since he's had so much.''

Charmaine sank down on the rust-colored sofa opposite the desk with a pouty look. ''I'd hate to be forgotten.''

Nadine regarded her dolefully. ''You've never been overlooked by any man in town yet.''

''I know that,'' Charmaine stated matter-of-factly. ''But the dance is fun.''

''Now didn't we agree that our *fais-dodo* days are over?'' Nadine chided.

''I guess we did.''

''That was a desperate move to help a desperate man. If that hadn't brought Will around, we would've had to get official help.''

''I knew he'd snap out of his slump,'' Charmaine declared with airy authority. ''Men usually respond to sensuality, no matter how down-and-out. We weren't out in his yard five minutes that first time, and he was already wearing his driving glasses.''

''A closed chapter to all concerned,'' Nadine stated with no-nonsense finality.

Charmaine sighed, allowing her robe to fall open as she crossed her long legs. There was no point in concealing her costume now—the chiffon scarves cleverly sewn into a bodice-hugging dress with a multilayered skirt that took flight with twirling movement. Nadine was well acquainted with the garment, having sewn it and another for herself at the old Singer sewing machine standing three feet away from the desk. Dancing Will out of his depression had been Charmaine's idea, but she'd known enough to leave the design and assembly of their dresses to Nadine.

Given a notion, Nadine reminded herself with pride, she'd always proven extremely creative and determined, nicely complementing her sister. And just like her sister, she sure had a notion about Jake. Jake was to be her man and that was all there was to it. But it was important that his child not be overlooked. She was determined to drive that fact home to Charmaine.

"Well, I suppose I'll go to bed," Charmaine announced, moving to rise.

"I'd like to discuss Amy Jo for a little while longer, if you don't mind," Nadine proposed, rising from her small springy chair. "She has a lot of needs right now."

"That's obvious!" Charmaine exclaimed, recrossing her long bare legs. "A feminine touch is sorely missing from that pitiful girl's life."

"Well, yes," Nadine conceded slowly, moving out from behind the desk. "Yes, but a gentle touch is most important."

Charmaine's forehead puckered. "What are you getting at?"

"Jake and Will are probably the only people on earth she trusts," Nadine went on to clarify. "She needs to feel she's the number-one female in their hearts right now.''

Charmaine fluffed her hair discontentedly. "A woman's touch could bring all of them joy!"

"But it has to be done subtly," Nadine argued. "You can't hope to take more than you're bound to give in return.''

"I wouldn't!"

Nadine clucked in reprimand. "Charmaine, clamping yourself to Jake like a human suction cup this afternoon was openly threatening to the girl. She is only eight years old. And her daddy is her hero, her everything!"

"She must've seen her folks hug and kiss," Charmaine argued. "It's natural.''

Nadine gasped at her sister's nerve. "You can't hope to slip into Rosemary's place that way!"

"Well, maybe I did overdo it," Charmaine admitted slowly, "...it being Jake's first day back. But that dang Rosemary won every race we ever ran, then finally ran right out of town with the man I wanted!" She socked her palm in frustration.

Nadine shook her head in amused tolerance. "The poor thing's passed on, Charmaine. It's high time you declared yourself the luckier one!"

"I see Rosemary in her daughter though," Charmaine confided. "In those huge brown eyes, full of wariness as they fall on me.''

"To be fair, both of them gave you that look only when you were in Jake's arms—Amy Jo today, and Rosemary so long ago.''

"And what did Jake look like, Nadine?" Charmaine demanded excitedly. "Was he happy to be kissing me?"

"He was...surprised, I think," she honestly replied.

Charmaine nodded in satisfaction. "That's a beginning. He knows better than to expect the expected from a Jordan.''

Nadine folded her arms across her chest and rocked on her stockinged feet. *My thoughts exactly, sister. My thoughts to a T.* With a smile, Nadine bade her sister an airy good-night.

Nadine was tugging up the yellowed shades on the high-paned windows of her classroom the following morning when Mildred Brooks appeared in the doorway. Nadine had chosen a casual white eyelet blouse and navy pleated shorts for this off-hours visit to the school. Not surprisingly, the tall, reedy principal was dressed with characteristic formality in a charcoal suit, her steel-colored hair secured in a bun.

''How nice of you to come in on a Saturday.'' Miss Brooks offered the clipped compliment as she moved into the room.

''I'm always happy to help out a student,'' Nadine returned brightly. ''I—'' Her voice caught in her throat as Calder and Thelma Parnell marched in behind the principal. The town's leading citizens wasted no time stepping into the foreground, to confront Nadine with stiff spines and flinty eyes.

Nadine watched Miss Brooks bend nearly in half before the couple in simpering admiration, then offered a more conservative greeting of her own in the form of a nod and a smile.

''We hear you are testing the child today,'' Calder announced, a blend of curiosity and annoyance in his tone.

''They would've appreciated more than an hour's notice,'' Miss Brooks said accusingly to Nadine. ''You should've called them directly with your plans.''

"Had I planned to include you, I would have," Nadine replied, bypassing the irritating Mildred to speak directly to the couple. "As it is, I don't think we need an audience."

"You mustn't forget all the Parnells have donated to our school," Mildred oozed on sharply. "I always feel I owe our biggest benefactors consideration."

A stranger would have to be told they were the town's most affluent couple, Nadine decided, assessing them with a far more critical eye now that they were giving Jake a hard time. Calder was a short, paunchy cherub type, with jowls that drooped lower with every passing year, just as the ring of hair on his head grew thinner and thinner. Tall, willowy Thelma, with her brown hair twisted into a shiny topknot, still had her looks. Many considered her an older, more faded version of her late daughter. Both of them were dressed in sportswear from Savannah, Calder in a bold plaid shirt and dark twill pants, Thelma in a white skirt and pink chiffon blouse. Nadine pursed her lips together. Their casual attire might just as well have been black judge's robes, for the autocratic stance they were taking, supposedly on Amy Jo's behalf.

"My concern is for one small girl," Nadine staunchly insisted.

"We understand that, dear," Thelma assured her sweetly. "We are on the same side, obviously! And appreciate anything you can do for our granddaughter. Don't we, Calder?" Thelma prodded, elbowing her husband's girth.

"Yeah, sure," he muttered impatiently, rubbing a hand over his mouth. "But we are equipped and anxious to take care of our own."

"What Calder means to point out," Thelma brightly

attempted to rephrase, "is that your goal matches ours. Amy Jo deserves the best of everything and shall have it. You're bound to be important in the scheme of things, Nadine—according to Judge Trimble. So we suggest you approach this matter with the wise sort of consideration you're known for."

"We do believe you to be wise," Calder added with an oily charm.

So they were hoping to woo her to their corner with sugar rather control her with vinegar. Nadine grimaced. Why not treat Jake that way? As angry as Nadine was, she couldn't help but pity them. They were so bent on control, they never delved beneath the surface of things.

"I have already outlined Amy Jo's obvious weaknesses," Mildred Brooks broke in, anxious to retain her authoritative status.

"You shouldn't have filled their heads with preconceived notions," Nadine gasped in surprise, ready to defy her superior to keep the record straight.

"Notions?" Miss Brooks flushed profusely, shocked by Nadine's uncharacteristic impertinence. "I have not only seen her, but spoken to her."

Nadine swallowed hard, trying to think of something the Parnells wouldn't care to argue about. "I am betting that the girl's likeness to her mother goes deeper than her looks, that she is just as quick, too."

"She looks like my Rosemary?" Thelma asked hoarsely, bringing an unsteady hand to her throat.

Mildred Brooks inhaled sharply, as though Nadine had committed a sacrilege. "No one could hold a candle to Rosemary Parnell. Certainly not that ragamuffin who's never enjoyed the Parnell influence!"

"Then your memory is failin' you, Miss Brooks." Jake's deep masculine voice sliced through the room, silencing the argument. Everyone whirled to look to where he filled the doorway, with a trembling Amy Jo flanked against his bulk, looking like a slender elf in yesterday's baggy jeans and loose flannel top. "My daughter is the image of her mother. A second angel on earth."

Thelma raised her chin high, struggling to maintain a dignified front as she gazed upon her granddaughter for the first time. "We wish to meet our granddaughter."

Nadine watched Amy Jo with a measure of pity. She was welded to Jake's length, her black, rubber-toed sneakers firmly planted on the floor. He had to hook his hands under her arms and lift her in the air to transport her into the room.

Nadine could see open disapproval clouding the Parnells' faces. She begrudgingly had to accept that her shallow sister had made a valid point last night about Amy Jo's appearance being as important as her studies—so important it seemed, that it should've been dealt with first. If Amy Jo had a trendy hairstyle and clothing this morning, everyone would've been been more likely to give her and Jake the benefit of a doubt.

To give Jake his due, he introduced Amy Jo to her grandparents in innocuous tones. Nadine knew it had to be excruciating, facing them after all this time and resenting them for being so narrow-minded back when their support was so desperately needed.

As for the Parnells, it was common knowledge they felt that Jake had stolen their daughter away from them. Irrational as it was, they believed that she'd be alive today if she'd lived her life in Cherry Creek.

There were bound to be emotional blazes from both camps. Nadine was determined to make sure Amy Jo didn't get singed.

Only minutes passed as the little girl faced her grand-parents, but it seemed like hours. Nadine was pleased to see Thelma bend to take Amy Jo's hand in hers, but Thelma's mission proved to be an inspection of the child's unevenly chewed fingernails. Calder stood over-head, frowning at the child's ever-present cap. The air was crackling with unexpressed hostility.

"I think it's time we get to work," Nadine announced briskly. "Sit down over there, Amy Jo, where I've set out paper and a pencil."

Jake gave her a gentle push forward. Amy Jo shuffled over to a desk, tugging the bill of her cap over her eyes.

"How nice of all of you to stop by," Nadine said in firm dismissal as she moved to the blackboard and picked up a piece of chalk from the wooden tray.

The adults clustered close to Nadine, out of the child's earshot. "Perhaps we can wait in your office, Mildred," Calder rumbled.

"Surely not for any results," Nadine protested with a short laugh. "I won't know anything for at least a week."

"I could settle this thing on my own a lot faster, Na-dine Jordan," the principal hissed in her ear.

Nadine smiled wanly, openly unaffected by the threat. "Judge Trimble is relying on me to give my report at the hearing," she whispered. "So like it or not, this is out of your hands."

With a withering look to her subordinate, Mildred Brooks offered to see the Parnells out of the school. The Parnells obliged, oozing with saccharine farewells to Na-dine and Amy Jo. The moment they were gone, Jake came up behind Nadine and set a hand on the gentle slope of her spine.

"That old crone hasn't softened a bit in two decades," he muttered close to her ear.

She turned to face him. "I know. I'm sorry."

"The Parnells were all sweet to you," he muttered darkly, restraint cording his neck.

"Playing it smart is all." She quietly explained about her part in the upcoming hearing.

"You can't be swayed their way, can you?" he whispered bleakly.

Nadine was torn between slapping the doubt from his rigid jawline, or kissing away the worry lines from his troubled eyes. She settled for a bland smile.

"I'll pretend you didn't ask," she sassed softly, turning to outline a basic arithmetic problem on the board. "Just know that we'll have to work quickly to put Amy Jo on her best footing."

"What can I do to help?" he asked in a nervous hush.

Nadine continued to run her yellow chalk on the smooth black surface, all the while aware of his hand at her waist, resting near her hipbone as though it belonged there. She inhaled shakily, wishing she could twist flush against him and kiss him on the mouth the way Charmaine had yesterday. But the temptation subsided as she took to heart some of the advice she'd given her sister concerning Amy Jo's needs.

"Well, Nadine?"

Nadine took a fortifying breath. "Go, Jake. Leave us be."

He cast a sidelong look at his daughter. "She won't appreciate it. Doesn't like being left, since her mother…"

"That's understandable," Nadine answered softly. "But it's clear that you've been meeting her needs all alone and—"

"And failing?" he cut in tersely.

"And must be tired," she corrected. "You've come back to town for help, so take it!"

"All right...." As he shifted from one foot to the other with a fluid shrug, Nadine couldn't help watching the play of his chest muscles beneath his tight green T-shirt, and found it a struggle to keep her eyes above the waistband of his jeans.

"What's goin' on?" Amy Jo asked belligerently from her desk. "You talking about me?"

"We're through talking." Nadine nodded meaningfully at Jake.

"I'll sit in the back and not make a sound," Jake bartered hopefully.

Her green eyes twinkled stubbornly. "Go knock around town, Jake. Have some coffee at the café. Maybe take a look in the Buttons 'n' Bows window for some spring things."

He wrinkled his brow. "That's a ladies' shop."

"I know," she said, shifting her eyes in Amy Jo's direction.

"Oh." New awareness crossed his features. "Guess she does need some prettier things."

"You don't have to go inside alone. We can meet you over there in an hour or so if you like," she suggested.

His gray eyes grew stark. "Nadine, please let me stay...."

"Please trust me," she murmured. "I know how to teach."

"Okay," he agreed on a heaving breath, and turned to address his daughter in a clear, bright voice. "So long, Amy Jo, I have some errands to do in town."

"Now?"

His face cracked with a halfhearted smile. "Yes, now."

Amy Jo squinted suspiciously. "Like what? Grandpa's got plenty of food."

"For one thing, you need new spring clothes," he blurted out desperately.

"I want to come along!" the child cried angrily, pounding on the desk.

"We'll meet your daddy in town after our work is done," Nadine promised.

"Good idea," he hastily agreed.

"No, Daddy, no!"

"Bye, Jake," Nadine prodded lightly.

"Bye, ladies."

"Daddy! Wait!"

Nadine swallowed hard, so proud of Jake at that moment. He lifted a hand in farewell on his way out, but he didn't look back once, or take a misstep. He was putting his trust in her and was encouraging his daughter to do the same.

Nadine turned back to Amy Jo to find she'd broken her pencil neatly in two and was holding the ends in tight red fists. She knelt on the floor beside the child and, raising a gentle hand, peeled the baseball cap from Amy Jo's head. A thick black cap of hair tumbled into the little girl's face.

"Give me that back!" The pencil pieces clattered to the floor as she reached out for her hat. "It's mine! I need it!"

Nadine was shocked at the child's vehement reaction. She'd hoped the cap wasn't a security blanket, but evidently it was just that. "Of course it's yours," Nadine assured her, setting it atop her own head. "It's a shame to hide such beauty, that's all."

"That's a lie! It's like that old lady said," Amy Jo cried out in a frightened bitter rush. "I'm not pretty like my mama, or as smart!" She made a lunge for the cap, and Nadine tipped over on the floor and had the breath knocked out of her. They rolled together in the aisle as Nadine gasped for breath. Amy Jo gave a frightened peep and her small face was sheeted in fear as her nose grazed Nadine's. They blinked at each other in amazement.

"You mad at me?" the child whispered.

"Yes," Nadine scoffed gently, easing them both to a sitting position on the scuffed gray tiles. "But only because you believe what Miss Brooks said is true."

"Oh." Amy Jo hung her head and stared down at their tangled legs.

"She doesn't have children of her own and sometimes doesn't use the kind of compassion she should."

"Oh."

"I imagine of lot of people have told you that you're pretty without the cap," Nadine ventured to guess, reaching to tip Amy Jo's chin so their eyes met.

"Some," the girl mumbled.

"And smart as a whip," Nadine pressed.

"Maybe." Amy Jo released a small sigh, and Nadine wrapped an arm around her shoulders. When Amy Jo yielded to the gesture, Nadine felt confident in pulling her close. "You think my grandparents like me at all?"

"I'm sure they do," Nadine murmured into Amy Jo's mussed hair, recognizing the scent of Will's pine-scented shampoo. How could he let the child use that gunk!

"But I'm not as good as my mama was," she wailed against Nadine's chest. "It's like that old lady told them!"

"Your mother was lovely and kind," Nadine con-

ceded. "But you are special in your own way, Amy Jo.
You have some of her traits and some of your father's,
too. A very nice blend by the looks of things."

Amy Jo's forlorn eyes gleamed with new hope.
"Think so?"

"Absolutely. Now wouldn't it be nice to show your
daddy just how smart and clever you are? Think how it
would make him smile."

Amy Jo lifted her face with a sniffle. "I suppose."

Nadine took a tissue from her shorts pocket and
handed it to her. "And your Grandpa Will is so looking
forward to seeing you settle in."

The child blew her nose and nodded.

"And you have Charmaine and me, too," Nadine
added. "We all want to help you, honey."

Amy Jo's thin black brows jumped in hope, then fell
again. "But I don't know any kids. And I don't talk like
you do."

"Your speaking voice is quite delightful," Nadine objected. "We'll find you some new clothes, and you'll be
amazed how easily you fit in."

Her brown eyes were shimmering with tears, but Amy
Jo managed a small smile. "Think Daddy will be waiting for us?"

Nadine sighed with relief. "I know he will. What do
you say we get the work out of the way so we can go
play?"

# 3

"Hey, Jake. I swear you've got your nose pressed against that glass like a little boy at the toy store!"

It was Charmaine's flirty voice floating along on the warm morning breeze, Jake realized with delight. He turned from the pane stenciled with pink scalloped letters spelling Buttons 'n' Bows, to the prettier distraction moving up the sidewalk in a royal blue, body-hugging cap-sleeved dress.

A slow, appreciative grin brightened his lean face. He'd been in town for ten minutes and had been wishing for some pleasant company to help ease him back into the town's rhythm. Talk about a dream come true! Charmaine was the perfect goodwill ambassador, with enough hip-swinging rhythm to shoehorn even the most unfavored son back into the fold.

Jake quickly realized that the pretty legal secretary's appearance wasn't acknowledged by him alone. Cherry Creek's downtown consisted of one long block of businesses sandwiched side by side in one-and two-story buildings, so it was easy enough to see everyone on the street all at once. Every male head had turned at the lilt of her voice, even the ones with females hooked to their arms or encumbered by packages.

"I didn't mean to startle you," she called out sweetly as she overtook the bakery next door to the dress shop.

His firm lips curled mockingly. "Course you didn't."

Charmaine tucked her clutch purse under her arm and sidled up close to see what had caught his eye behind the glass. He shuddered slightly as the curve of her breast grazed his biceps. Was it an accident? The catlike cunning in her eyes verified that it was quite deliberate. So she was interested. But to what degree?

Jake controlled his growing grin with effort. It would be so satisfying to prove to Will that he knew his Jordan women. In town a day and he already saw great promise in both of them; Nadine would play the doting mentor to his daughter and Charmaine would play the flirty vamp to him. It would make it all so easy for him. And didn't he deserve it, after all the tough times he'd endured?

"I love presents," Charmaine gushed longingly as she studied the feminine items on display. "Ruby Davis knows how to dress up a window, doesn't she?"

Jake's heart slammed against his rib cage as she slanted her gaze to a shimmering red teddy laid out on a fringed white pillow, then back to him with a naughty hazel twinkle. She was coyly inviting him to picture her in that scrap of lace and satin, sending him a clear signal that she had some serious sexual play in mind. Perfect! Just perfect... Remembering that they were on a public street, he winked in understanding, then focused on some of the tamer items, like some T-shirts and sunsuits that Amy Jo might fancy.

Charmaine, never known for her patience, began drumming her long tapered nails on the glass in a persistent raindrop patter. He found himself hypnotized by her fingertips, coincidentally polished the same scarlet shade as the teddy. The teddy that was made for Charmaine, with its bodice that plunged forward and bits of lace that would hide nothing...

He was allowing himself to be seduced in public, at ten o'clock in the morning! he realized suddenly. It was ridiculous schoolboy behavior. They weren't rowdy kids anymore. He was a twenty-seven-year-old father seeking a respectable place in the community, striving to provide a secure environment for his withdrawn little girl. Amy Jo would always come first. That was a condition that Charmaine would have to agree to from the start.

When the patter didn't draw him from his reverie, Charmaine turned her body flush to his and raised her hand to his face. "Is it possible to get your undivided attention for one measly minute? Can't we at least talk?"

Jake sucked in air between his teeth as she buried a single red nail in the cleft on his square chin. He grasped her slender hand in his huge one, carrying it away from the tender spot. "So what brings you to town, Sassy?"

Her lush mouth widened with pleasure. "Why, it's my habit to browse on Saturday mornings. Everybody meets on the street round this time." She squeezed his arm. "You know how I love people, Jake."

His gray eyes twinkled. "Yeah, Charmaine, I remember."

"Some more than others, of course," she added coyly.

Suddenly he realized that she was wearing her hair the way she had the night they'd almost made love in the back seat of Will's old Ford four-door. The thick honey-colored mane was woven into a loose braid that sliced the center of her back. Short wisps that had escaped the braid danced across her forehead in the breeze.

She'd been wearing blue then, too, and the same pearl pendant at her throat.

The bold manipulator wanted him to remember that night! Remember it and long for a rematch. She figured there was no one standing in her way this time. Naturally, Rosemary had been his choice back then. He'd resisted Charmaine's charms because of her. Deep in his heart, even at the randy age of seventeen, he'd known Rosemary was the one for him.

But it had been the purest form of carnal temptation. Charmaine had been every adolescent's dream date. And still was! Incredibly, her moves hadn't changed a bit in the past decade. No doubt she still got around.

Now Nadine... She'd been shy as a teenager, and from what he could see she had a shy, much more subtle approach to men than her sister. She would avoid the meaningless flirtations that Charmaine lived for. It seemed to him that the sisters' vastly different personalities hadn't changed—just as he had so shrewdly told his father!

Above and beyond all his expectations, he suspected that Nadine had remarkable depth, a bonus he was wise enough to appreciate. Rosemary, too, had possessed an inner strength. As his intelligent wife grew weaker with illness, she'd encouraged him to seek out other female role models for their daughter in the small scattered circle of their acquaintances. He'd failed rather miserably, in his antisocial, scared-stiff state. Nevertheless, he certainly wanted his daughter to grow up into more than a coy mantrap craving affection and approval. Rosemary would heartily approve of Nadine guiding Amy Jo.

But it was proving to be incredibly hard to think about depth, wisdom and parental guidance when he could feel Charmaine's slender hand stroking the inside of his upper arm. As sturdy as his limbs were from the construction trade, that area of skin remained sensitive. Leave it to her to remember his weak spots. And promptly put her knowledge to work. Nadine's sweet, trustworthy image evaporated from his mind as quickly as it had appeared, replaced by the very real lip-licking Charmaine. Hot tense seconds passed until he ultimately managed to draw a clean mental slate, but only after gently brushing aside Charmaine's touch.

"To be perfectly honest, Charmaine," he began on a sigh, "I'm browsing for some clothing for my daughter. She's been in her own kind of private mourning over Rosemary's death, and part of that has been denying her feminine side, playing the scruffy tomboy."

"Well, we can fix that," Charmaine chortled confidently. "You've come to the right place—the only place." She tried to tug him toward the glass door but Jake stayed rooted to the sidewalk. "C'mon, darlin'. I won't steer you wrong!"

"I'm just killing time out here," he tried to explain. "Nadine promised to come round with Amy Jo—"

"Oh, they might be over at the school for hours," Charmaine scoffed. "Nadine's like a mole, the way she burrows in over at that old smelly building, pouring over papers and books."

Jake looked around the bustling street and realized that people were watching them. This was partly because Charmaine was so easy on the eye, but they were also bound to be curious about his return and his troubles with his former in-laws concerning Amy Jo's custody. The town of two thousand didn't get this sort of soap opera very often—Cherry Creek's most affluent citizens battling last decade's football hero. With a sigh, he gave in to her.

Buttons 'n' Bows' proprietor, Ruby Davis, was thumbing through a side rack of spring dresses when they stepped inside. She called out a generic hello at the jingle of the doorbell, but didn't turn around. Charmaine replied, while Jake shuffled around, absorbing his surroundings. Like many of the establishments along the street, this one was decorated with pine-paneled walls and ceilings—courtesy of a huge sale at the lumber yard over twenty years ago. But there were only dribs and drabs of the pale wood showing through the vast assortment of stock Ruby kept on hand. Ruby's shop, providing garments for females of all ages, sizes and income brackets, was the closest thing to a department store that Cherry Creek had.

Jake nodded cordially at Ruby when she did spin round. ''Nice to see you again.''

''Why, Jake Flynn in the flesh!'' she exclaimed, her chipmunk cheeks bunching with a joyful smile. ''You look fine.''

Jake surveyed her as she bustled forward to give him a hug. Plump, jolly, gossipy old Ruby, in a rayon dress that boasted more ruffles than the white curtains on her door and windows, overdone with jet black curls and boldly penciled brows. He'd never known anyone more suited or satisfied with her job, forever cheerfully helpful and observant. The latter made her a very accurate quid-nunc; which, if you were destined to be one, was probably the preferable kind.

''So sorry to hear about our wonderful Rosemary,'' Ruby gushed kindly. ''What a comfort your little girl must be.''

''Amy Jo's the center of my world now,'' Jake confirmed, his heart warming with her genuine concern.

She bobbed her curly head. ''Don't know what I'd

have done without my Buddy after his dad ran out on us back in '76,'' she admitted bluntly, never so hypocritical as to conceal juicy tidbits concerning herself.

Jake stole a glance at Charmaine at the mention of their classmate, Buddy Davis. He was originally Leon Davis, Jr. But once Leon Senior hit the road, Ruby couldn't bear to hear the name anymore and nicknamed her son after a favorite uncle. Charmaine's eyes were alight with mischief, just as Jake expected. Will had informed him that, as expected, Buddy had grown up into the town's most prominent do-less, a counter hopper here in Buttons 'n' Bows by day, a hustler at the pool hall by night.

''Buddy's become indispensable around the shop,'' Ruby went on to boast. ''Since the Tailor Trader closed up last year, I've been handling some menswear, just so's the fellas don't have to go all the way to Savannah for socks and shirts and things.'' She gestured to a glass counter in a far corner under the fan. ''Works out fine having a male hand,'' she confided soberly. ''Bein' that some of the more modest men don't care for me to handle their underpants.''

Jake raised his hand to his mouth, struggling to disguise a blurt of laughter behind a cough.

Charmaine mercifully intervened. ''I understand you've even been cutting some hair back in the alley, Ruby.''

Ruby waved a puffy hand. ''Had to stop that, dear. Once I started dating the barber steady, it seemed trashy to undercut him in business.'' She chuckled over her own pun as she moved back over to the central counter holding her ancient cash register. ''So what can I get for you today, Jake? Perhaps you'd be more comfortable dealing with Buddy. He's just out back in the loading zone having a smoke."

"That's really unnecessary," Jake protested. "I—"

"No trouble," she insisted, parting the yellow gingham drapes concealing the stockroom entrance. "I can see him through the back screen door. "Buddy?" she hollered. "Buddy!" she repeated on a firmer note. "Come in here, I have a surprise for you."

Jake grimaced, pacing stiffly. He had no wish to waste his time sparring with Buddy. The do-less had always envied him his prowess in school sports and his luck with the girls.

Buddy barged through the curtains moments later dressed in a gray T-shirt and wrinkled black pants, a burning cigarette dangling from his mouth. His lips curled at the sight of Charmaine, then thinned when he spotted Jake.

"Hello, Buddy," Jake greeted simply.

"Heard you were coming back," Buddy returned, his voice still holding traces of a boyish whine. Jake noted that Buddy didn't appear to have expanded his horizons much at all. His pale brown hair was shaved close around his ears and topped with a longer thatch that fell across his forehead, in a style currently worn by males half his age. His shoulders were curved and narrow from lack of physical activity, and he had a potbelly, no doubt from Ruby's home cooking and pool hall beer.

"Ain't it nice that your old chum is back, Buddy?" Ruby prodded, snatching the cigarette from his mouth and stubbing it out in a tin ashtray near the register.

"Dandy, Ma," Buddy drawled. Resting his spindly forearms on the counter, he leered in longing at Charmaine. "How's it goin', Char?"

Charmaine tapped her foot on the plank floor and gave him a dismissive smile. "Fine, Buddy."

"You hungry?"

"Not particularly," Charmaine replied with a puzzled frown. "Why do you ask a thing like that in the middle of the morning?"

"Cause the last time I invited you to the Dixie Diner, you said you might never eat again," Buddy reminded her sulkily.

"Actually, Ruby," Jake cut in, "I'm here to shop for my daughter, and Charmaine's along to help."

"A whole wardrobe?" Ruby's beady eyes lit up like a slot machine flashing a jackpot combination. She gave Buddy a forceful shove of dismissal. "Go ahead, son, go back to what you were doin'."

Buddy's lip protruded. "You stubbed out the last of my smokes, Ma."

"Then go and get some more at the market. Make your manners over there to Mr. Foley and ask him to pack up my weekly order."

"But, Ma…"

"Get on now, Buddy," Charmaine urged, summoning Ruby to the children's section. "I believe we can handle this in no time at all," she enthused to Ruby. "Amy Jo is eight years old and about the size of Penny Hubbard."

Buddy's exit was marked by the slam of the door and a sharp clank of the bell. Jake sat in a white wicker chair beside the dressing room door while the women discussed options. He could see the sidewalk clearly from his spot, as well as the items in the window display. He let his mind wander as he watched the steady stream of pedestrians and vehicles through the large square pane. No matter how hard he tried to focus on the mundane, his eyes continued to stray to the sexy piece of lingerie

Charmaine had so boldly admired, bringing forth fresh erotic images that made his muscles melt with longing.

Jake rubbed his temples in a jumble of desire and despair. The seductive setup was almost more than a red-blooded man could take. And completely understandable, since he hadn't had a woman since Rosemary. After well over a year of abstinence, he was itched raw over Charmaine's open invitation. How delicious she would look in that teddy. He closed his eyes, surrendering briefly to a picture of her swaying up the gazebo steps in that satin scrap, her ivory body gleaming in the moonlight. After hearing his father talk of the *fais-dodo* the sisters did in the Flynns' backyard, Jake couldn't help but imagine how it must've been. He was certain that it hadn't been all that arousing, considering that Will had had his share of heart trouble over the years, so he allowed his mind to expand on the idea, until he sizzled right down to his toes. He couldn't help releasing a soft moan as Nadine's voice broke through the foggy fringes of his fantasy, as though she were trying to step into the picture. But that was silly. Not proper little Nadine. He tried to shake off her voice, but he couldn't quite manage it.

"Jake Flynn! Are you listening to me?"

His heavy eyes snapped open to find that fantasy and reality had merged for a very good reason. Nadine was standing before him in the shop, her hands on her hips, her eyes chipped emeralds. Lost in his daydream, he hadn't heard the bell jingle with her arrival.

"Hey," he offered awkwardly, hoping that her icy stare didn't drop low enough to spy the solid flesh straining his jeans. "Guess I dozed off for a minute or two."

"I thought you were going to consult me on this shopping spree," she fumed quietly. "Or at the very least, wait for Amy Jo."

"Well, I just happened to run into Charmaine on the street," he faltered, forcing eye contact to keep her gaze high above his belt. She'd never understand his condition, his desperation, his male needs. He'd die if she thought less of him for it.

Nadine shoved her hands into the pockets of her shorts, rolling her eyes to the pine ceiling. As if anything was an accident with her big sister!

"You can help," he offered. "Amy Jo would value your opinion above the others, I'm sure."

With a last trace of hope, Nadine swiveled on her heels, only to find that Amy Jo was already sandwiched between Ruby and Charmaine at the full-length mirror. They were fussing over the frail-looking child like two clucking hens, whisking garments in front of her with a flourish.

Nadine's heart sank. Amy Jo had been shy about obeying Charmaine's initial direction to join them, but apparently that had been short-lived. Sometime during Nadine's confrontation with Jake, the girl had slipped over to the other camp. She was now oblivious to Nadine, the one who'd comforted her, cajoled her into doing her best, being her best. How naive Nadine had been to believe that they'd just bonded in an exciting, significant way over at the school.

Nadine was fully aware that Jake was watching her curiously, waiting for her response. Again, she had to play it cool in order to avoid tipping her hand to Charmaine. But she couldn't completely disguise the hurt as she again faced Jake. "Quite honestly," she said breathlessly, "I don't think I'm needed here anymore."

"That's not so," Jake hastily protested, studying the

dark emotions playing across her pert and pretty face. What was going on in that clever little mind of hers? He realized with a jolt that Nadine wasn't as readable as she'd been at thirteen. Something he hadn't counted on, but apparently the price he'd pay for her spirit and intellect. If he didn't know her better, he'd swear she too was staking a primitive claim on him.

Just like Charmaine.

Will's caution concerning the Jordans niggled at him in his trap of uncertainty. Was the old man right when he suggested both sisters shared some mysterious, volatile, interchangeable traits? It seemed impossible! Nadine was very prim and proper back at the school, wielding chalk and pencils, giving directions.

But the way her fanny moved when she erased that blackboard of hers... Even under yesterday's loose dress, he'd detected a fluid hipsway that must have sent those second-grade boys reeling from day one on.

No-no-no! He put on the mental brakes right then and there. He had everything set in his mind. His risk-free future all mapped out. He'd stick to the set path and think no more about it.

His newly formed mask of indifference was enough to propel Nadine into reverse. "I have so many pressing errands," she stammered in goodbye, backing up in the direction of the door and nearly knocking over a rack of panty hose. "Like going over Amy Jo's tests, and... other very important things."

She was gone in a flash. Jake's jaw sagged as he absorbed the encounter. Any fool could see that Nadine was deeply hurt. Maybe he should've tried harder to stop her. Better yet, he should've waited until she arrived, as agreed. That would've kept this shopping incident simple and innocent, and out of murky emotional waters.

He never would've been caught with a hard-on, and never would've caused that crazy dazed look on Nadine's face.

The bottom line was that Amy Jo needed Nadine and Nadine deserved his faith and respect. He'd make it up to her, he vowed. When he purchased the teddy for Charmaine, he'd get Nadine something real nice too.

# 4

"**E**verything smells great, Dad!" Jake enthused the following day as he peeked into all the pots and kettles simmering on the stove. Will shooed him away as he slid a pan of biscuits into the oven, but not before Jake caught a glint of pleasure in his father's smoky eyes. "Just like old times," he added, "having the Jordans over for Sunday dinner."

"Have to start Amy Jo off right with our favorite traditions," Will agreed, patting the girl's dark head as she passed by carrying five green ceramic plates. "The Flynns and the Jordans taking the noon meal together seems like a good start."

A reminiscent smile played across Jake's features, softening the lines set there by strain and sunshine. Lavish meals like this one, of fried chicken, biscuits, black-eyed peas and onion pie, were commonplace while he was growing up. Served here or next door on a rotating basis, he couldn't begin to count the times he'd drawn comfort from the memories of those meals. They'd given him strength throughout Rosemary's illness, and were now giving him the courage to battle the Parnells for the right to head his own family.

"So what's on your mind, son?" Will asked, studying Jake's expression with interest.

"Oh, just wondering how you and your *fais-dodo* friends have managed without me all this time," he bantered back with a wink.

Will's chuckle was cut short by an indignant sound from Amy Jo. They turned in surprise to find that she'd lingered in the doorway to eavesdrop. "Why, what's the matter, sugar?" Will asked in a gravelly, perplexed voice.

"What about my mama? Didn't she come over here? Didn't she count? What about her folks? Those Parnell people seemed all right."

Will and Jake exchanged an awkward look as Amy Jo shot questions at them in an anguished voice, her soft cornflower eyes now blazing blue fire. Rosemary had come over on the occasional Sunday, but it was a rare and covert move on her part. The affluent Parnells wouldn't have approved of their daughter mixing with the Flynns. Even before all hell broke loose over the romance that had joined their families, Calder and Thelma had barely managed a tolerant nod at the half-Cajun Will and his wife Jolene on the street. Will was a plainspoken carpenter who provided services for the Parnells' kind. At best they would've laughed over their simple, modest food and dinnerware, or scoffed at their old dining room table, which had been showing its age fifteen years ago with scratches from the Jordan girls' patent-leather shoe buckles and Jake's experiments with woodworking tools.

Amy Jo was waiting for an answer, Jake realized, with her small chin jutted, her lower lip trembling, the heavy plates sagging in her hands. The morning had been so cheerful up to this point. Thanks to Charmaine's shopping choices, his daughter was dressed in a white shorts set with pink pinstripes, her black hair glossy from a new, gentler shampoo. She'd brightened noticeably when Jake and Will had complimented her on her appearance, and her happiness had carried on into their biscuit preparation. She'd looked so much like her mother as she carefully cut circles in the rolled-out dough, disregarding the dot of flour on her nose. Jake had found himself caught up in a bittersweet joy, relishing the moment, wishing Rosemary could share it.

As it was, the best he could hope for was that Rosemary was keeping an eye on them from the heavens, and was behind his campaign to forge ahead in a fresh direction.

What to tell Amy Jo? She didn't know anything yet about the Parnells' prejudice against the Flynns, or their battle to win custody of her. Everyone had kept things cordial in the classroom yesterday, and it was bound to confuse her. He'd tried to tell her many times, but she already had so much to bear for one so small.

"Well, Daddy?" she asked in a small husky voice.

Jake crossed the worn green linoleum, dropped to one knee and steadied the plates in her hands. "Of course your mama came over, baby," he soothed with a smile. "It was just that we were closer to the Jordans. They lived next door, and Ned and Myrna Jordan enjoyed our company." Jake broke off at a loss for a way to explain the situation. He was eternally grateful to hear Will shuffle up behind him.

"Rosemary and her folks lived outside of town on their fancy farm," Will added easily. "Had fancy friends to enjoy."

"Those Parnells came to look at me yesterday," Amy Jo asserted in bewilderment. "You think they want a grandchild like me?"

Jake's corded body stiffened. His voice fell flat, despite his efforts to behave neutrally. "I'm sure they would."

"Mama cried whenever she talked about 'em," Amy Jo challenged in confusion.

Jake grimaced with shock. He and Rosemary had tried so hard to keep their unhappy legacy from their daughter.

"Sometimes adults have disagreements," Will told her, scratching his bristled chin. "But that doesn't concern you, Amy Jo."

All three of them gave a start as the back screen door squeaked and the Jordan sisters entered on a cloud of laughter and sweet perfume.

"Could be twins standing there," Will greeted jovially, with a nudge to Jake, still on his knee. "The prettiest pair in the whole wide world!"

Jake grinned. Will was a crusty old cob, wily enough to again point out that the sisters might be more interchangeable than his son believed. Jake had to admit they appeared especially similar today, dressed in sundresses that displayed their creamy shoulders, with their luxuriant blond hair twisted into French braids. Charmaine wore a print dress that highlighted the gold and green in her eyes; Nadine had chosen a rosy red that drew out the strawberry in her hair.

The most important thing was their feminine presence, he told himself, rising to his feet as Charmaine steered Amy Jo through the swinging door leading to the dining room. Will followed, asking them to dig a tablecloth out of the sideboard. The kitchen fell silent as Jake wheeled around to find himself alone with Nadine.

The air was electric with an energy that Jake couldn't define, and it understandably left him shaken. Amazingly, Nadine didn't seem to share his bemusement. She wore a confident little crook of a smile that was nothing short of purposeful.

"Made a jam cake for you, Jake."

The announcement was sultry, sweet temptation, oddly disconcerting and comforting to him all at the same time. He watched Charmaine's little sister waltz over to the counter and set her mother's old tin cake pan down beside the sink. He closed in with roguish anticipation. "Blackberry jam?"

"Uh-huh. With brown-sugar icing," she added in a skittish rush as the soft fabric of Jake's crisp white shirt grazed her bare back. She longed to lean into his solid length, revel in his strength, listen for his groan of desire.

Feel his erection nudged into the small of her back.

She couldn't stop thinking about his obvious arousal in Buttons 'n' Bows yesterday. He'd been daydreaming about something or someone, when she'd jolted him to life. He'd just about exploded out of that creaky wicker chair of Ruby's! And he'd looked so guilty, tucked away in that corner by himself. It had appeared that he was mooning over that extravagant red teddy no one in town had the nerve to buy. Or was it just wishful thinking on her part? It was a mighty big leap of imagination to think that he was envisioning her in that lingerie. But she couldn't help hoping. Surely he wasn't completely oblivious to the effect he was having on her!

"Dad and I appreciate you girls coming by," he murmured in her ear.

Girls? Couldn't he appreciate her alone, think to take advantage of this moment they had together? A pang of irritation simmered in her belly when she felt nothing but a belt buckle digging into her skin. A small sign of encouragement would mean so much. Charmaine was already so sure of her position as the chosen sister. She'd boasted on and on last night about how she'd clothed Amy Jo like a beautiful doll, then taken her to the drugstore to get appropriate toiletries, and how they'd lingered at the fountain for chocolate sodas. Charmaine had sworn that Amy Jo had so thoroughly enjoyed the adventure, she'd behaved like a little girl with a bright new outlook. Charmaine's message had been clear: Amy Jo was strong enough to welcome a woman into the family circle. And naturally Charmaine believed herself to be that woman.

Jake hovered near, savoring the light lemony cologne at Nadine's throat. A pretty girl and jam cake, the perfect dessert for a Sunday in spring. He'd unconsciously wedged her between his thigh and the counter, and now found himself reaping unexpected rewards. Lord, her bottom was firm. The short coarse hair beneath his black denims stood on end in animal response. "Never had teachers like you when I was in school," he uttered in awe.

Nadine stared out the window at the dark green hedge of Cape jasmine that ran along the black fencing dividing their properties, intent on hiding the flicker of annoyance flaring in her eyes. He sounded so helpless and bewildered, it lessened her enjoyment of the compliment. But it was a start, wasn't it? This could even be construed as her chance to turn around and kiss him thoroughly, just as Charmaine had done on Friday. Light his fire so that he was rock hard from head to toe.

In the seconds to follow, Nadine thought better of it. She simply wasn't the type to force such a response from a bewildered man. And his mixed signals were confusing the daylights out of her. This just wasn't good enough. She had to be certain they were on the same wavelength before making a move for intimacy. If an impulsive kiss were to upset him, make him doubt her levelheadedness, he just might not entrust Amy Jo to her care. And Amy Jo desperately needed her sound maternal guidance. Flighty Charmaine might be a good mother someday, but she would do well to work her way up from a newborn babe, grow along with the child. Amy Jo needed practical support here and now.

Though decidedly on her guard, Nadine couldn't pass up the opportunity to encourage Jake in the right direction. She pulled her nail through the icing on the cake, and as she turned ever so slowly, pushed the sugary cream toward his mouth. His gray eyes widened in surprise, but his tongue flicked over her fingertip with a deep groan of appreciation.

"There are so many things I've missed around here," he confided huskily.

"What do you want, Jake?" she asked in a tentative whisper, drawing her finger around to his prominent jawline.

"To win my daughter free and clear," he automatically replied.

She tapped his nose with her moist finger. "No, silly, for you. As a man with dreams of his own."

"Oh." The question jarred him, but not enough to loosen his deep dark secret. On such a warm, sunny afternoon it would be wrong to tell this pretty young thing that his dreams had already been fulfilled and taken away, that the best was over.

"Jake?" Nadine was squeezing his arms with gentle expectation, waiting for his answer. He couldn't help but be flattered that she cared. It almost made him wish he had a meaningful personal goal.

"Well, I suppose what I want most right now is someone to make me blackberry jam cake,'' he declared with a boyish grin.

Nadine flushed with pleasure, encouraged to say something about her own dreams, when a rap on the back door interrupted their conversation.

Jake edged away from the sink, aware that Nadine was on his heels. He didn't recognize the stocky blond teenage boy on the stoop, dressed in cutoffs, carrying a vase of white roses, but Nadine did.

"Hello, Billy!" she greeted in cheery surprise. She edged past Jake's solid form and opened the screen door. "What brings you over here?"

"These are for you," Billy announced, setting the vase in her hands. "When I got no answer at your place, I decided I'd try here."

"Thank you!" she cried in delight, burying her face in the snowy petals with an appreciative sniff. "Everybody knows your father's greenhouse is closed on Sundays, though," she suddenly recalled.

"Calder Parnell paid Dad triple to open up and deliver his order today," Billy reported, openly puzzled. "You must've done something mighty wonderful to please that old bugger."

"More like you're expected to *do* something mighty wonderful to please that old bugger," Jake muttered in her ear the moment Billy loped off. "Like give Judge Trimble a fancy line about how Amy Jo belongs on the Parnell peanut farm."

"You should be happy that the judge is a fair man who can't be swayed by the Parnell name," Nadine huffed indignantly, setting the vase on the table with a thump. "And surely you don't think I can be bribed, do you?"

Jake batted the air, barely missing the tops of the

blooms. "I know you're as fair-minded as you are pretty, honey," he growled. "But...well, we both know Parnell's a man who can give you the sun and the moon if he wants to. Being rich, he has the option."

Nadine pressed her lips closed, swallowing back the lump in her throat. In her eyes, Jake was the one who held the sun and the moon in his hands. Even as a budding young lady, she'd felt there was a special chemistry between them, sensed that Jake was everything a good man should be. More than anything, she wanted to help him set his world in order, and have him discover that she was the perfect mate for him. So far, all he wanted was jam cake! Funny, she didn't remember his being so dense, so flat-out stubborn. Why, the poor bumbler needed her more than he could ever comprehend!

"The idea that I'd ever recommend the Parnells as parents over you is ridiculous!" she finally managed to blurt out crossly. *Even if you end up choosing that flighty sister of mine, I'd never do it.*

He seized her suddenly, clamping his hands around her waist. Nadine emitted a tiny squeak as he drew her against his sturdy length. This was more like it! she inwardly rejoiced. His taut body was humming with excitement, his eyes were silvered with emotion.

"I'm sorry I'm so short-tempered," he rasped.

Nadine's lips curved, forming a moist, luscious pink half-moon. "Don't ever apologize for expressing a real feeling, Jake. Not to me, anyway." She wondered if he was going to kiss her then. His huge workman's hands were still at her sides, kneading her tender middle through the snug-fitting bodice of her dress. She wondered if he knew how potent his seductive powers were, if he understood that pushing his thumbs into the edges of her navel was sending lightning through her system, reducing her limbs to jelly. She dazedly searched his troubled features for an answer. He seemed lost, unsure what to do with her. Oh, how she longed to show him!

The spell was swiftly broken a moment later when Will charged back into the kitchen, hollering for them to stand aside from the oven, scolding them for not smelling the burning biscuits.

Will managed to save the biscuits amidst the tangle of helpers and commotion. Nadine attempted to disguise her raw desire by grabbing a striped dish towel and swishing smoke through the open window. She felt their burning intimacy being carried away on the spring breeze, as well, but there was no way to stop it.

Naturally Amy Jo noticed the vase of roses. "Where did those come from?" she asked in a happy singsong, burying her nose in the petals just as Nadine had done.

"They're from the Parnells," Jake curtly explained.

"For all of us?" Amy Jo wondered, her blue eyes wide and soft.

"Why, certainly," Nadine assured her, arching her brows at Jake's growing scowl. Though it would make Thelma and Calder appear a bit more generous than they deserved, it was the only way to save the child's feelings, wasn't it?

Feeling a stronger flare of temper this time, Jake withdrew to the back stoop and focused on a cluster of robins zooming through the trees. He flinched when the screen door creaked again and he felt Nadine crowd in behind him on the small block of concrete.

"You understand, don't you?" she whispered, gently touching his shoulder blade.

Jake slowly swiveled on his heels. "They are the enemy, Nadine." Her features crumpled under his terse admonishment, but he couldn't bring himself to soften.

Didn't she see he was fighting for his very life here? That little girl was his everything!

Nadine steepled her fingers in a prayerlike position. "Amy Jo needs all the family she can get—"

"You and I put one foot wrong before Judge Trimble and these Sunday dinners might be all I have left with my own girl!" he said harshly under his breath. "I can't bear another loss, Nadine. I can't ever lose my girl."

"The Parnells are misguided, spoiled by too much power, but they are decent deep inside," she attempted to point out. "They've done a lot for the town over the years—"

"A minute ago you seemed to be on my side a hundred percent," he challenged in dismay.

"I am!" she assured him. "But when all is said and done, and you've had your day in court, Calder and Thelma will still be the grandparents in the background. Amy Jo is too young to be at war with kin she doesn't know—"

"I'll make that decision," he cut in furiously, clenching his fists.

"It is possible to watch your back during this feud and still manage to keep a small corner of your mind open..."

"Maybe from your objective viewpoint it is. But Rosemary's pain is still so vivid in my mind, Nadine," he attempted to explain. "Do you think she enjoyed being abandoned by her parents? Do you think it was easy convincing her that she wasn't to blame for their stupidity? I spent the entire course of our marriage trying to make up for the void they left. And believe me, we had a lot on our own. The Parnells weren't needed then or now."

Nadine understood all of that. And she was impressed

with Jake's love for his late wife. How wonderful it must have been, even for such a limited time, to be cherished and protected by him. But he was jumping to so many conclusions that could hurt both him and Amy Jo. She decided if he wanted her support, he'd have to simmer down and roll with the punches. "Fine and good, then," she said with forced equanimity, "but there is no reason for you to carry this attitude to the table. It's our first reunion meal, and Will has worked so hard. If you let the Parnells spoil it, you'll be hurting everyone, yourself most of all."

He reared back with furious disbelief. For a moment, she wondered if she'd gone too far. Finally he exhaled, making a visible effort to calm down. "Yeah, teacher, I should know better than to carry my anger into the best of times."

"Then do better," she advised with a grin, opening the screen door wide.

The dinner that followed was a delightful scene out of the past in so many small ways. Her parents and Jolene were missing and Amy Jo was a new face at the table, but not much else had changed, Nadine thought as she savored forkfuls of Will's sweet, creamy onion pie.

Will, seated at the head, with his dark wiry arms propped on the table, still pointed his fork at whomever he happened to be addressing, and punctuated his remarks with a laugh that seemed to erupt deep from the hollow of his chest.

Charmaine, ever conscious of her figure, was rearranging the oversized helpings of food set before her by Will, just as she had when their parents were present. She was still trying to divert attention from the ploy with silly stories about Buddy Davis's undying adolescent love for her, and about the more colorful clients from Len Tyler's law office.

Jake dipped biscuit after biscuit into the gravy on his plate as though he were still on his way to football practice. But while he'd once been known to focus a good ninety percent of his attention on Charmaine, he now divided it among everyone around the table in a more mature way.

Amy Jo occupied her time tasting the dishes foreign to her palate, before beating her father to the last biscuit. She was responding to all of them with new vibrance, Nadine noticed, and was as pretty as a picture in her new outfit.

"Did you tell the ladies that we're going to be painting the house this week, Jake?" Will queried during a lull in the conversation.

"Not yet," Jake replied.

"Len Tyler thinks you'd better get a real job fast," Charmaine inserted, taking a dainty sip of ice water. "Before—"

"Charmaine!" Nadine gasped in warning. Will had alerted them to the fact that Amy Jo wasn't to know anything about the custody battle until the time came.

"Before what?" Amy Jo piped up in bewilderment.

"Why, before I run out of money," Jake promptly replied. "You'll be happy to know, Charmaine, that Dad and I are planning to start up a little home-improvement business here in town. A nice new look to this house will be good advertising."

"Exactly right," Will seconded, winking at Amy Jo. "All we need is an expert to pick a color."

"Well…" Charmaine trailed off, puckering her painted lips.

"He means Amy Jo, sister," Nadine took pleasure in pointing out.

Charmaine's delicate jaw dropped, as understanding chuckles rose. "That's fine," she said with a sniff. "I was simply going to point out that exteriors are not my specialty anyway."

Amy Jo propped her chin in her hand and crunched her small face in thought. "I always wanted to live in a yellow house," she announced. "With green shutters. Real bright, like the sun and the grass."

Will's narrow chest shook with laughter. "That would stop traffic."

"Is that bad?" Amy Jo asked, nibbling nervously on the last biscuit.

"Not at all," Will assured her, despite Jake's leery expression. "I'm sick and tired of bland white anyhow. About time we jazz things up."

It was over jam cake and coffee an hour and a half later that Charmaine pushed herself into the spotlight by suggesting that Amy Jo show off some of her new outfits.

Amy Jo swallowed a mouthful of cake with a dubious look. "Nobody wants to see all that stuff. Do they?" she peeped hopefully.

"Of course we do," Nadine promptly encouraged.

"C'mon, then! We'll dash upstairs and give 'em a show." Charmaine bounced out of her chair, grabbed Amy Jo by the hand and tugged her through the sitting room to the open staircase. "We won't be needing you, Nadine," she paused to add with an insincere smile that didn't do much but deepen the dimples in her flushed cheeks.

"I know you won't," Nadine conceded with a tolerant smile and airy wave of her knife.

Jake sat back in his ladder-back chair, cleared his throat and sipped from his green ceramic coffee cup. He eventually gazed across the table at Nadine. "I hope the way things went yesterday at Ruby's place hasn't left you out of sorts over Amy Jo's wardrobe."

"A happy ending for Amy Jo is the most important thing," Nadine assured him evenly, tearing at the paper napkin hidden away in her lap.

"It's not that you weren't needed," Jake persisted, "not at all."

"I know." She fidgeted in her seat, wishing they could move beyond her wounded-doe dash out of Buttons 'n' Bows.

Jake smiled in relief. "I think you'll agree that Charmaine and Ruby managed. I saw some of the things spread out on her bed this morning and they looked fine."

"Well, the candy-stripe shorts and top she's wearing today is just right for her," Nadine managed to say.

"Charmaine never does a thing halfway," Will put in with dancing eyes, leaning forward in his chair to take another slice of the dwindling cake.

Nadine's mouth thinned. Charmaine was all flash as usual, the main attraction with minimal effort. But it was her influence that would set the child on the right path. Why, it was even her cake that Will was eating! She suddenly realized that they were watching her dark expression with interested surprise. "If anything needs alteration, I'll be more than happy to oblige," she lamely offered to offset her irritation.

"You are quite handy with a needle and thread," Will praised, settling back with his treat. "Those were the prettiest dresses you girls wore for the *fais-dodo*." He shoveled in cake with a guileless expression, as though such a situation were as commonplace as a campfire sing-along.

Jake gave him a disapproving frown. "Maybe now that you're so chipper, Dad, you'd like to start up a nice little romance with a local widow."

"Too busy," the old man objected. "I've got my garden, my woodworking projects, and now our handyman venture besides. It's true I enjoy a flirty show from time to time, but that's enough for me. It's you, Jake, who should be shining around the ladies."

Nadine raised her napkin to her mouth to conceal her sudden blush, forgetting that it was in shreds. Luckily Jake was reddening himself, and too occupied with his own discomfort to notice.

Nadine dropped the ripped square back in her lap as though it were aflame and the threesome polished off their dessert in silence.

Charmaine and Amy Jo reappeared minutes later, alive with laughter and murmured secrets. Jake swelled with pride at the sight of his daughter. Amy Jo glowed, with her rich black hair woven into a French braid like the sisters wore, and her skinny form set to feminine advantage in a full-skirted, butter-colored dress.

Nadine regarded the scene with horror. She had seen this particular dress, with its ruffled hem and bows trimming the waistline, in Ruby's shop window some weeks ago. It had been reduced a few times, then finally removed from the display. It was vintage Ruby, the sort of thing the blowsy, self-appointed fashion queen of Cherry Creek would try to push on all the youngsters in town. Being a naive newcomer, Amy Jo would've been the perfect pigeon on which to unload old stock. *Ancient* was actually a better word. This particular style hadn't been worn by grammar school girls since Charmaine herself had fluttered her lashes and petticoats on the playground! Nadine pursed her lips, on the verge of exploding with frustration.

By the time the pair reached the dining room, Nadine had managed to assume an air of casual nonchalance. And none too soon. For despite Jake's expression of faith in Charmaine, he was openly looking to her for approval. And so was Amy Jo, who shifted from one patent-leather shoe to the other, reminding Nadine of a miniature version of Scarlett O'Hara, full of spunk and vim, with a twinge of uncertainty deep inside.

Nadine took a sip of coffee and set her cup back down with a clank. They'd let Charmaine barge in and run wild with Ruby, and now they expected practical little sister to validate their lingering doubts. Why, oh why hadn't Jake stuck to the plan yesterday? Why had he let Charmaine butt in?

"Isn't she the prettiest little girl you've ever seen, Nadine?" Jake prompted, his gray eyes flashing a silent plea.

"I made that observation on Friday, the moment I laid eyes on her," Nadine evaded with a smile.

"He means now, Nadine, in the dress," Charmaine pressed, twirling her finger to instruct the child to do a pirouette.

"I can remember Rosemary looking very much like that on any given Sunday," Nadine softly replied as the child did a full turn on the hardwood flooring.

"You sound like my daddy, Nadine," Amy Jo noted with pleasure.

Charmaine frowned and grasped the child's rail-thin shoulders, determined to control the scene. "Would you like to show off another dress?" she suggested excitedly.

"Would you like to see another one?" Amy Jo asked them tentatively.

Nadine nodded with an encouraging smile. "Very much."

The pair scurried off again chattering.

Jake cast a fond look after his daughter, then turned back to face Nadine. "Talk about tiptoeing around on eggshells. You couldn't have said less if you tried."

"I preferred not to lie," Nadine confessed apologetically. "I did find Amy Jo quite lovely at first sight on Friday, despite her hobo appearance. And she does look very much like Rosemary in that dress."

He drilled her accusingly. "Still, you don't approve!"

Nadine sighed, clasping her hands together on the table. "All right, I don't. If this dress represents the lot, we've got big trouble." She went on to explain about Ruby's ploy to clear old stock and the outdated image Ruby and Charmaine shared concerning ladylike fashion.

Jake listened, set his chin grumpily.

"You have to understand that Charmaine's point of view hasn't changed from the days she and Rosemary attended classes at Lincoln," she told him. "Up until now, until Amy Jo, the only youngster she's been friendly with is the muscle-bound delivery boy over at the market." Nadine's lips curved wistfully. "It's harmless, of course. She simply likes to watch his biceps bunch when he carries our grocery bags."

"I used to be that delivery boy," Jake mumbled, rubbing his eyes.

Nadine nodded. "Yes, I know. To her, a lot of things are just like they used to be."

Jake felt dizzy and lost. It was obvious that Nadine was warning him that Charmaine hadn't expanded her horizons in a number of areas. But the elder sister was still so appealing in a basic, sexy, self-centered way. Regardless, he'd have to be more alert in the future, make sure the right sister was consulted for the right task. If Charmaine wanted to play him for the besotted fool, well, it might be a whole lot of fun. But Amy Jo was another matter. It was crucial that she not come up short because of any adult blunders.

"Jake, you should've known better," Will scolded. "This is just the kind of mistake the Parnells can use to cast you in an incompetent light."

"I know they didn't dress like that in Cleveland, but I thought maybe they still did here," he offered in feeble excuse.

Will snorted without pity.

"So what do you propose we do?" Jake demanded. "C'mon, Nadine, I need you desperately."

Nadine's pulse quickened under his attentive gaze, and she couldn't help pretending that he yearned for her, and not just her advice. "Let's hope the first dress was a fluke," she suggested hopefully.

"Let's assume the whole bundle is a washout," Jake amended with practicality. "Then what?"

Nadine sighed. She knew what had to be done, but she really didn't want to do it.

"Please, honey," he rasped.

Her thick lashes swept over her creamy cheeks in a deliberate attempt to break eye contact. Her mind was busily searching for options. There had to be another way. There just had to be!

"Seems to me if the clothes are wrong, they have to be returned to Buttons 'n' Bows," Will inserted. "And the money used for proper ones."

"That's exactly right," Nadine agreed absently, far

ahead of him. "It's just that the shop is closed Sundays like most everything else."

"Then Jake will take action first thing tomorrow," Will said adamantly.

Jake's eyes grew. "I don't want to haggle with rambunctious old Ruby! Everybody in town knows a sale in that place has always been final."

"Ruby's responsible, though," Nadine objected. "If she tried to pull a fast one, she'll have to take the things back. You can go first thing in the morning, Jake, and quietly arrange for credit. I'll stop by with Amy Jo after school and start the selection process all over again."

"What about tomorrow, Nadine?" Will asked urgently. "She needs an outfit for her first day. Would the shorts set she wore to dinner do?"

"Too skimpy for the classroom," Nadine declared, causing the men to groan in chorus. She should be the one groaning, she realized. She would have to make things right, while Charmaine got off scot-free—as always! "Tell you what, I'll alter something," she forced herself to say. Naturally that brought smiles to their faces!

"Tell me what I can do to help," Jake prompted. "There must be something…"

Nadine compressed her mouth. Now came the tough part. "If the next outfit is awful, we can be fairly sure the lot is bad. In that case, it would be nice if Charmaine were distracted for a while, so I could go up, survey the damage and calmly explain it all to Amy Jo."

"Guess I could manage some distraction all right," Jake offered with shameless anticipation as they heard sounds on the staircase again. "Give me a little kick under the table if you want me to take her out," he added in a hasty conspiratorial whisper.

Nadine smiled grimly. What better motive for a good swift kick!

Charmaine and her small model appeared in the arched doorway once more. Nadine nearly choked as she tried to swallow back a gasp. This dress was actually worse than the first! Sheer peach nylon fabric flocked with daisies, cinched at the waist with a wide satin belt, with a straw hat to match. Damn that Ruby! Damn Charmaine! And damn her own sense of duty!

Jake murmured her name and she reluctantly shifted forward in her chair to meet his gaze. He was moving his brows, waiting for a sign. She promptly gave him one, whacking his shin hard with her white leather shoe. As a reluctant cupid, she couldn't help but feel that misery did indeed love company.

# 5

"**W**hy couldn't I go to the drugstore for a soda with Daddy and Charmaine?" Amy Jo was asking Nadine the question for the umpteenth time as they surveyed the wardrobe laid out on the child's quilted bedspread.

"Because I need you here with me," Nadine reiterated simply.

"But it don't make sense," Amy Jo whined, flailing her skinny arms.

"Doesn't make sense," Nadine automatically corrected, drawing her fingers through her thick mane. This was the moment of truth that she'd so artfully arranged. Jake had spirited Charmaine away on a wave of intimate laughter.

Nadine exhaled as she relived their arm-in-arm exit. She'd felt an incredible sense of loss when Jake's broad back and lean hips had moved through the Flynns' front screen door behind Charmaine, and across the wooden porch fronting their white saltbox. His taut shoulders had loosened with every step, as though his troubles were evaporating into thin air.

And why shouldn't he feel his burden lightened? Free of parental pressures for an hour or two, strolling off with a high school sweetheart, all the while confident that good old Nadine would set things right.

If only she could be in flighty Charmaine's place for a change, making mistakes but still managing to reap the rewards for no good reason. Now that she was sure Jake was the man for her, she desperately wanted to show him her secret, sexy side, the reckless edge of her personality. Give him the kind of show Charmaine had intended Friday night—a sizzling, spontaneous *fais-dodo* in the shelter of the Flynns' backyard gazebo. Shock the living daylights out of him, set him right, once and for all.

But all this was just a whimsical dream so far, for Jake didn't seem to see beyond her caretaker role. It was a role that was bound to keep her busy for a while, too. There was the wardrobe to contend with, then the even more important scholastic issue to tackle. Judging by her low test scores, Amy Jo wasn't going to be able to complete the second grade without some tutoring. Nadine figured she had a week to help the child bring her grades up, the amount of time she told the Parnells she'd need for testing. She'd have to find a way to break this news to Jake. There hadn't been a free moment yet to tell him.

"Nadine helped me decorate this bedroom for you, Amy Jo," Will announced jovially from the doorway, jolting Nadine back to reality.

Amy Jo, once again dressed in her candy-stripe outfit, surveyed the bright cheery room full of muted blues and pinks with a toss of her head. "You told me that yesterday, Granddaddy," she informed him huffily. "I want to know what's going on here. I keep askin' her, but she won't tell me."

Nadine rubbed her temples as she turned her back to the source of the trouble. Every article of clothing on the mattress had lace, right down to the crisp white anklets. She caught Will's eye and gave him a thumbs-down signal. Amy Jo, in the meantime, had stomped over to join her at the bed, with her spindly arms crossed on her flat chest.

"Something wrong, Nadine?" she asked in a cooing, patronizing tone that she'd most likely picked up from Charmaine. "You seem out of sorts today. Your sister thinks maybe you wanted to help us and felt left out."

Nadine leaned over and pinched Amy Jo's chin. "How like Charmaine to say something so silly."

"She says a lot of funny things," Amy Jo praised. "She acts like my friends back home."

"That's no surprise," Nadine retorted over Will's deep chuckle. "You seem a lot happier for it and I'm glad."

"Of course I'm happier," Amy Jo replied pertly. "Charmaine promised that I'll be very popular in school, with all my new clothes and my hairdo. I look nice, don't I?" she queried earnestly. "You all said so."

"You are pretty and sweet," Nadine answered, and Will, who had moved into the room, rumbled agreement.

"Then what's the matter, Nadine?" Amy Jo asked gently, touching her arm. "I really like you a lot, too."

Nadine's insides melted as she looked down into the child's huge blue eyes, framed with the longest black lashes she'd ever seen, save for Jake's. She sat down on the edge of the mattress and pushed aside a chiffon blouse to make room for Amy Jo. Nadine angled an arm around her as the little girl dropped down with a bounce. "Do you remember what I said over at the school the other day, Amy Jo, about being on your side?"

Amy Jo shrugged. "Yeah."

"Well, sometimes bad news is for your own good."

"I don't want any more bad news!" she flared, attempting to bolt up.

Nadine squeezed her shoulders, keeping her firmly in place. "It isn't that bad," she consoled. "Is it, Will?"

"Naw," Will scoffed with a wave of his rough copper-colored hand.

Amy Jo's eyes threatened to fill. "You just tell me and we'll see how bad it is!"

"I thought she took the whole thing very well," Nadine told Will on an upbeat note down in the kitchen thirty minutes later.

Will set a second mint julep before her, then popped the cap off a second bottle of beer for himself. "Amy Jo can't stay locked in the bathroom forever, I reckon," he said with a philosophical sigh. "At least I hope not. Another beer and I'll have to impose on your hospitality next door."

"No," Nadine shouted, pounding on the table.

Will's jaw sagged at her blunt refusal to share her facilities. "Huh?"

"If anyone goes next door, it will be the ladies," she explained with new determination. "Enough is enough. Amy Jo's mopping the floor with me in a way I don't let my students do. And we're wasting precious time. I need to get her into one of those dresses so I can measure and get the alterations started."

His faded eyes began to twinkle. "I imagine a nail would pop that door easily enough."

She nodded soundly. "My daddy used that trick more than once."

Amy Jo didn't appreciate being ousted from her porcelain haven, but Will was adamant about taking her place. Nadine watched the exchange from across the hallway in Amy Jo's room, where she was packing things back in pink paper sacks bearing the Buttons 'n'

Bows name. She was flooded with relief as the girl stomped inside to join her.

"Well, go on and pack up everything if you're going to take it away," she wailed. "I'll just hide in here forever and ever and never go to school!"

"If you'd have let me finish before, I'd have told you that your daddy and I have this all figured out. I'm going to fix up one of the dresses for tomorrow, and he will return all the rest."

Amy Jo's eyes widened in horror. "He won't know what to buy me!"

"Simmer down," Nadine soothed with a flutter of her hand. "He'll do the returns and we'll go in after class and start out fresh."

The plan obviously made sense to Amy Jo, for she quickly ran out of steam. Her delicate features smoothed into good humor and her breathing returned to normal. "Won't Charmaine be mad?"

Nadine blinked, amazed at how quickly her sister had made her mark, after the rocky start with the kiss she'd given Jake. "I promise I'll explain it all to her so she'll understand."

Amy Jo lifted her frail shoulders with a sigh. "Okay."

"Now come give me a hug and we'll choose a dress that can be saved with a needle and thread," Nadine urged with her arms opened wide.

Nadine held her breath as Amy Jo hesitated. But only a heartbeat passed before the child stumbled into her arms like a newborn calf on wobbly legs. Nadine squeezed her with pure pleasure, realizing that she felt much more than a duty here; she wanted Amy Jo's love as much as she wanted Jake's.

It was nearly nine o'clock when Nadine finally heard a mingling of Jake's masculine laughter and Charmaine's high giggle floating on the night air. Seated at her sewing machine in the second-floor study, where she was putting the finishing touches on Amy Jo's revamped dress, Nadine couldn't help popping up to peer through the window screen facing Simpson Street.

Sure enough, they were just coming up the uneven walk together. The golden glow of the front porch lamp and the white rays of moonlight blended to illuminate them. Jake's white cotton shirt stood out, as did Charmaine's bright print dress. They'd obviously picked up an intimate rhythm during their walk, achingly evident from Nadine's bird's-eye view. Their legs and hips swayed in sync with every step. Charmaine had unbraided her hair at some point, for it was now an unruly mass of spun gold as she tossed her head back with sultry laughter.

Nadine balled her fists. Charmaine had used the time alone with him wisely, was already moving in for the seductive kill. If Charmaine could bed him tonight, she would. No available red-blooded man could be expected to resist her sultry big sister under these romantic conditions. It was up to Nadine to make sure he wasn't put to the ultimate test and taken out of reach for good!

Nadine's heart and hands raced as she frantically severed the two threads tying the dress to her machine. She gave it a final once-over, deciding that it looked quite nice. She and Amy Jo had decided to work with the butter-colored one she'd modeled at dinner. Together they'd made it an adventure, and with some careful pinning and clipping had stripped the dress of unnecessary detail. Gone were the puffy sleeves and the ruffles and bows, leaving a sleeveless shift with a slight flare at the hip. It was simple, but not overly so. With any luck, Amy Jo would ease into the school day without incident.

At sundown she'd finally insisted that Amy Jo go home and get a good night's sleep, promising to deliver the dress sometime later in the evening. How lucky that she was still working on it. It gave her the perfect excuse to disrupt the lovebirds.

Nadine bounced down the staircase with the garment slung over her arm and landed in the front foyer. She moved to the coat closet and swung open the door to view herself in the full-length mirror concealed on the inside panel. She hastily undid the braid holding her hair, just as Charmaine had done, then fluffed her red-tinged tresses over her shoulders. The front of her scarlet dress was a bit wrinkled from her time at the sewing machine, so she attempted to smooth it with long sweeping strokes. She would've liked to change into something else altogether, but she didn't have time. The porch swing was already creaking, and their voices had dropped to a more intimate level.

Nadine's appearance was heralded by the creak of the old wooden screen door. The couple on the swing instantly fell silent, making Nadine's stomach knot. Were they already concealing things between them, as lovers were bound to do? Or was it just a natural pause to include her? She sauntered over to the slatted white chair suspended from the porch ceiling in the cozy dark corner among the hanging baskets of begonias and caladiums.

It was easier than she anticipated to force a smile to her lips. Jake wasn't touching Charmaine at all. She was cuddled up close to him, the folds of her dress frothing over his thigh, but he didn't have a hand on her any place. He gave her what seemed to be a genuine smile in greeting.

"Shame on you, Nadine!" Charmaine breathed on a high-pitched squeal, jabbing a long talon at the small butter-colored dress.

"I broke the news to her about the wardrobe," Jake needlessly added.

Nadine's insides melted as he flashed even white teeth at her with a conspiratorial wink. There was a spark in his eyes for her alone. Charmaine didn't own him inside out yet!

"The idea that I don't have a connection with children is just plain nonsense!" Charmaine sputtered in affront.

Nadine placed a hand on her hip. "Charmaine, give it up. Children are my life. Why, just my presence in the classroom every day gives me vivid insight into their needs. This fashion thing was my turf."

"I'm trying my damnedest to figure out both your specialties," Jake intervened with a chuckle. "Guess I just need more practice."

Recognizing a derisive note in his voice that was bound to completely escape her sister, Nadine leaned over and gave his solid shoulder a nudge. "You better watch your step, mister. Nothing's ever as it seems."

Jake made a deep satisfied sound, amusement dancing in his eyes. "A lesson my daddy taught me."

Despite her confusion over the content of the verbal sparring, Charmaine recognized a flirtiness in Nadine's moves. Big sister was openly mocking as her carefree laughter rang out like a clear little bell. "As if Nadine is a danger to anyone over the age of eight!"

"In that case, Charmaine, you won't mind if I speak to Jake alone for a minute," Nadine said. "About Amy Jo," she added silkily.

"I suppose not," Charmaine said with airy confidence, rising from the swing in a graceful motion. "I have to call Len tonight yet, anyway. See if he needs me in the office first thing in the morning.''

Jake watched her hip-swinging exit with admiration. ''Night, Sassy.''

She paused halfway across the porch, peeking over her shoulder. ''Night yourself, sexy.''

Nadine thought the screen door slammed shut behind her sister a bit harder than necessary, but it was little more than a fleeting observation as she eased into Charmaine's vacated spot on the rocking swing.

''So what's on your mind?'' Jake inquired gently, fondly, forever anxious to set things right for his daughter.

''First off, I want you to know that Amy Jo is in good spirits despite all the commotion. And I'm fairly certain she'll fit in fine tomorrow.''

Jake relaxed visibly and angled his arm behind her as she set the dress in his lap. ''Thank you, honey.''

Excitement tingled through Nadine's system as his roughened fingertips pressed into her tender upper arm. She couldn't resist leaning into him a little bit, turning her head to study his profile. Light poured in from the two large living room windows beside them, illuminating every angle of his face. She suspected the tenderness softening his features was a blend of friendship and gratitude. Such feelings could be channeled into love and desire, she was certain.

''If I didn't know you better, Nadine,'' he murmured into her strawberry-blond tresses, ''I'd suspect you were trying to seduce me.''

''I wouldn't put anything past a Jordan sister,'' she cautioned lightly, raising a delicate hand to his cheek.

His mouth quirked at the corners. ''Another lesson my daddy taught me.''

Nadine fidgeted as heat softened her thighs. Will must have told him about the *fais-dodo*. Naturally, they'd done it with the most sterling of motives, feeling that the end justified the means. Will knew that full well and wouldn't pretend otherwise. Still, it was encouraging to know that Jake understood that she could dance around his backyard in a bit of silky nothing if she felt like it.

It was all coming together, she could sense it. Why, he'd even brought up the question of seduction himself! In a teasing tone of disbelief, granted, but it was a start. If only she could follow through. Again, it wasn't the proper time. "I'm afraid it's Amy Jo's academic standing that's on my mind right now," she confessed with reluctance. She immediately felt his muscles tense.

He cleared his throat. "When you didn't say anything after the testing, well, I assumed—I hoped, anyway, that things were all right."

"Well, I was going to tell you at dinner today, but the time was never right. Amy Jo is a bright child," she rushed on, dropping her hand to his wrist. His pulse was leaping wildly. "She will need some tutoring to catch up to the other second-graders, though. I will be more than happy to help, of course, to teach her privately, at night if you like."

The swing creaked as he shifted his weight. "Does she know yet?"

"No," Nadine replied with surprise. "I wanted to confer with you first, make sure you agree with my judgment before she's involved."

His thick arm tightened around her. "Oh, Nadine, of course I trust you," he crooned. "You could have told her on your own."

Nadine closed her eyes for a brief moment, hoping to hide the wanton gleam heating them. This closeness was exquisite torture. She was increasingly aware of a hungry sensuality gnawing at her insides.

"Nadine?" he ventured on an uncertain note. "Please believe that I'm totally in your hands with these things from here on in. I won't give you another minute of trouble like I did at Ruby's. Whatever you say goes."

Nadine smiled dreamily. "You won't be sorry, Jake."

"Don't get all power mad," Charmaine interrupted succinctly. "You've lived too sheltered a life to teach that girl everything."

Nadine snapped her eyes open to find her sister just beyond the living room window, kneeling on the blue velvet sofa, with her forehead puckered and her mouth set grumpily. Charmaine was a cautious female first and foremost, Nadine realized. Despite her lack of faith in Nadine's sex appeal, she'd lingered to spy. Nadine sought to keep the mood frivolous to throw her off the scent. "Hope you freeze that way," she teased.

Jake's rich chuckle added to Charmaine's consternation. "I'd still be the prettiest girl in town!"

"Perhaps you should go speak to Amy Jo, Jake," Nadine suggested, ignoring her sister's vain declaration. "Now, before she's asleep."

"Excellent advice," he concurred.

"There's all kinds of lessons and all kinds of teachers," Charmaine said in sultry protest. "Don't you forget that, Jake Flynn." With that she flounced out of sight.

Jake sighed. "Charmaine still has to have the last word, I gather."

"Charmaine still has to have whatever she wants," Nadine retorted.

His mouth curled in the shadows. "I have the feeling that doesn't stop you from having your share anymore,

Nadine.'' His eyes flicked over her length in open appreciation. ''It's more than obvious that you've come into your own.''

Nadine regarded him in coy silence. Someday soon, Jake Flynn. Someday soon.

Jake was a little uncomfortable as he walked through the center of town Monday morning with the bright pink Buttons 'n' Bows sacks tucked under his beefy arm. He got a couple of whistles from the old loafers seated in front of the barber shop, and a few honks from farmers passing down the main drag in their old pickup trucks, but it didn't faze him enough to wish he had Amy Jo at his side to carry the bags. Nadine felt that haggling with Ruby over the returns would put further stress on his daughter, so he was more than willing to handle it alone.

On Nadine's advice, Jake had spoken to Amy Jo about being a bit behind the other children academically, and about allowing Nadine to tutor her. Amy Jo had been upset. She wondered why it had happened to her, if she was dumb, what her late mother would think of her being behind, and if Nadine thought less of her. In retrospect, Jake realized that it was right they hash out the issues alone. Amy Jo needed reassurance that she was his only priority and needed the freedom to be completely open, even about the Jordans.

Somehow Nadine had sensed all this in advance and pointed him in the right direction. How quickly she was proving indispensable. If she had Charmaine's sensual nature, she'd be well-rounded perfection.

Ruby Davis was in the process of unlocking the front door for business as Jake strode up to her white brick shop. As usual she was dressed for an Easter parade in a busy print of colorful flowers, her inky hair rolled in thick curls, her lipstick a red slash across her pudgy powdered face. She called out a jovial hello as she caught sight of him, but grunted at the sight of his re-bundled purchases. Jake easily recognized her panic and was quick to wedge his solid shoulder between the curtained door pane and Ruby to ensure admission.

Ruby teetered on her chunky legs as he wheeled past her to the cash register, but moved quickly to the central counter and eyed him challengingly. "What can I do for you today, Jake?"

Jake set the bags on the glass surface beside a tarnished bin of plastic barrettes, noting that Ruby was pushing her cuffed sleeves up her sturdy arms as though squaring off for battle. "It's not as bad as you think, Ruby."

Ruby's beady eyes shifted warily despite his good-humored demeanor. "I have a no returns policy here, always have. And, quite frankly, after all the time I spent outfitting your daughter, I figured you'd be the last customer who'd be dissatisfied—"

"Ruby, Ruby," Jake said gently, patting her pudgy white fist. "This is an exchange, nothing more."

"But an exchange on everything?" she demanded in exasperation.

"Nearly so," he conceded. He attempted to open the nearest bag, but she was way ahead of him and took over the unloading.

Ruby shook her head as she pulled out the frilly garments one by one. "Surely with the lovely Charmaine's help, I did right by the girl."

"It was my error in choosing the wrong sister for the task," Jake admitted as Buddy emerged from the curtained doorway behind Ruby, dressed in his lifelong uniform of tattered jeans and misshapen striped T-shirt.

Buddy stepped up behind the broad expanse of his mother, leering beneath a fringe of floppy brown hair. ''Can't imagine anybody ever considerin' Charmaine wrong for anything. Can you, Ma?''

''No, I cannot!'' Ruby heartily seconded. With a patronizing smile, she leaned into the counter as though to share a confidence. ''You know, Jake dear, Nadine is a kindly teacher, but being cooped up in that schoolhouse all the day long with youngsters and spinsters, she doesn't know diddly squat about fashion.''

Jake hated Ruby's attitude but had every intention of outsmarting her with some shameless ego pumping. ''You're a worldly woman with a big heart to match, Ruby. It's clear that you and Charmaine are strictly cosmopolitan in your outlook. But that doesn't wash over at the school. Amy Jo's little classmates aren't ready to follow your more sophisticated lead.''

''I should say not!'' Ruby bellowed, pounding the counter. ''You hit the nail right on the head, Jake Flynn. I've been trying my darnedest to reintroduce a more genteel way of dress to the children of Cherry Creek to no avail.''

''Well, call it sheer ignorance if you will,'' Jake murmured with a conciliatory smile. ''I'm sure you'll understand that Amy Jo's not ready to blaze a fashion trail. Losing her mama was awful, and she would like to blend in with her peers at this time.''

Ruby's bosom heaved underneath the strained fabric of her print. ''What do you want to do, Jake?''

''I want you to tabulate my credit. Nadine intends to stop by after school with Amy Jo and start this shopping spree all over again. Okay?''

''Well...'' Ruby scrunched her puffy face. ''Goes against my policies. Would be financial suicide if folks saw me weaken my stand. In a burg like this, you can't recycle things much. People know what other people buy.''

''I won't tell a soul,'' Jake solemnly promised.

''All right,'' she conceded, and reached into a drawer at her thick waist for a pencil and tablet of paper to total the sales tags.

''I would also like to buy a couple of gifts while I'm here,'' he added, noting that her beady eyes instantly brightened. ''I could use some advice.''

''How nice!'' she gushed. ''I suppose that Buddy can handle the ciphering. Buddy, take this in back and come up with a total.''

Buddy gave her a peeved look. ''But you told me to unpack that carton of slippers, Ma.''

''Oh, I did, didn't I?'' she recalled in syrupy apology. ''You go on ahead, then.'' She stuffed the pencil into her crown of lacquered curls, prepared to give Jake her undivided attention. ''Let's sort out the buyin' first. It'll do my heart good.''

Jake inhaled, irritated that Buddy was obviously lingering to eavesdrop. The do-less had shuffled over to the carton brimming with satiny slippers but was taking his sweet time removing them from their plastic sleeves and setting them on the pyramid-shaped shelf. ''I'd like to get something for the Jordan sisters,'' Jake turned to tell Ruby.

''Like a set of towels?'' she asked. ''I've got some pretty ones with a lily appliqué that they could set out for callers.''

''No, something more personal,'' he explained quietly. ''Something for each of them. Two separate gifts.''

''I see,'' she tittered in understanding. ''Your interest in one is...uh...different than in the other.''

"They have different natures," he corrected, irritated with her presumptions, plain tired of her altogether. "I am grateful to both of them for their help with Amy Jo and for being so good to my father. I simply want to reward their hospitality."

Ruby adjusted the bracelets and rings on her fingers with an impatient sigh. "I don't have a notion in the world about what you're looking for," she finally said in loud exasperation.

This scene was turning into a nightmare, Jake realized, grinding his teeth. How foolish of him to think he could discreetly buy Charmaine the teddy she'd admired in the window the other day without having Ruby make a production out of the sale. And he sure as hell wasn't expecting the no-account Buddy to be still hanging around his mother, eager for something juicy to happen.

The bell over the entrance jingled suddenly and an older woman Jake didn't recognize entered babbling about the sunny day and the fact that she was in desperate need of a new girdle for a trip to Savannah. Ruby invited Jake to browse while she assisted the woman.

The pine-paneled walls of the cramped, overstocked shop seemed to close in on him as he sauntered round examining blouses, dainty handkerchiefs, scented soaps and the towels that Ruby had first recommended. The teddy captured his attention with every 360-degree turn, tempting him, teasing him, reminding him of his basic, burning desires, dormant for too long. He glanced surreptitiously at Buddy, who was balanced on his knee, gripping a pair of pink slippers like a pathetic Prince Charming.

Buddy smiled slyly, noting that his mother was chattering across the room, paying no attention to either of them. "Seen you looking at the underwear in the window."

Jake raised his brow indolently. "Did you?"

Buddy cackled. "Real purdy stuff, ain't it?"

"Yeah."

"Dated Charmaine back in school, didn't ya?"

"I dated a lot of girls back then," Jake hedged.

"Seems only right that Charmaine be mad at you for choosing Rosemary over her," Buddy reasoned on a whiny note.

Jake's features turned to granite. "Charmaine isn't the vindictive type."

"No, she ain't," Buddy agreed with a pensive sigh. "She's a real sweetheart. Deserves the best man in town." He tapped a slipper on his chest before setting it on the shelf.

Ruby moved up behind them then, the huge faux stones twinkling on her fingers. "I'm all yours again, Jake. Have you made up your mind?"

"He wants that red underwear in the window," Buddy announced with a self-satisfied look.

She was taken aback. "Is that so, Jake?"

"Well, I'm considering it," he admitted, rolling his eyes to the ceiling.

Ruby linked arms with him, making a cooing sound. "You have wonderful taste. That particular item came all the way from Paris, France."

All the way from Paris, Texas, more likely, he wagered with a rueful tug to his mouth. "Box it up for me, will you?" he blurted out, his courage fueled by his desire to escape. He strode over to the main counter with more purpose to examine its contents as she bustled around, eventually joining him with the teddy, two flat boxes and some note cards.

"I'll throw in the wrapping for free," she bargained as she began lining one of the boxes with tissue. "You decide on Nadine's gift yet? I am assuming that the teddy is for Charmaine," she added. When he frowned, she appeared insulted. "Talkin' to me is just as secure as talkin' to the pastor."

Jake paused, aware that anything too large would appear to be a bribe, an attempt to outdo Calder Parnell's pricy roses. And for the sake of his own sanity, he wanted to clarify her position in his life, clear up any confusion about where they were headed. "Maybe something like this," he said with sudden inspiration, tapping the glass case with a blunt fingertip.

Ruby bunched her chipmunk cheeks. "Perfect choice for a schoolteacher. And a practical one that will offset the outrageous price of the teddy."

Jake got his first look at the price tag on the scrap of flimsy lingerie as she arranged it in the bed of tissue, and gulped in horror. Money was tight right now. Paying off Rosemary's hospital bills had stripped his savings account nearly clean. And there was the new business with Will...

"Would you like me to subtract these things from Amy Jo's credit?" Ruby's question scattered his agonizing thoughts.

"No!" he erupted. "The idea never occurred to me." He extracted his wallet and paid her in full, realizing that his own worn clothing would have to last a while longer.

"Delivery's included with cash purchases," she told him. "If you're interested."

"Sounds fine, Ruby." Jake was so eager to go he almost forgot to sign the small crisp cards she'd set out for each package. As he picked up the shop pen tethered in place by a chain, he marveled that Ruby actually had the diplomacy to move away. He bit his lip as he searched for the right words. It was so important that he let each sister know just how he felt about her.

Nadine's was the tough one. How to let her know that he considered her an indispensable friend, a miracle worker with his fragile daughter? He labored over a brief message that he felt covered his feelings and tossed the card atop the artfully arranged gift.

He eagerly snatched up the second card, scrawled a far more provocative note for Charmaine and edged it into the soft gentle folds of the teddy, away from prying eyes.

"I'll take care of the rest," Ruby promised, popping the covers on the silver-coated boxes with a wink. "I'll just wrap a white ribbon round Nadine's and a red one round Charmaine's, so's I can tell them apart."

Jake cast a jaundiced eye in Buddy's direction. "You'll see that they're delivered properly, Ruby…"

"Don't you fret, dearie. I'm goin' by Len Tyler's law office later on anyway to drop off some custom-made shirts he ordered. And I'll make sure the other box gets to Nadine sometime this afternoon."

Buddy, still on his knees beside the pyramid shelving, watched Jake leave with a spring in his step. Flynn had always been so sure of himself, so lucky to be admired for no good reason. Buddy's pale eyes then shifted to his mother standing at the counter measuring lengths of red and white ribbon from the huge spools beside the register.

"Got to get this taken care of right," Ruby declared with a humph.

Buddy's thin lips quirked, thinking how much fun it would be to see something go wrong for his childhood nemesis. With deliberate clumsiness, he staggered to his feet and bumped into the pyramid. It fell with a noisy clatter, sending the satiny slippers across the slippery wood flooring like shiny missiles.

"Buddy Davis!" his mother shrieked, abandoning her wrapping project to charge across the store.

"Sorry, Ma," he squeaked with a feigned little-boy apology. As Ruby dropped to her knees to right the shelving, he wasted no time taking her place behind the counter. With a sly, swift motion he switched the boxes set upon the separate strips of ribbon. "Tell you what, Ma," he called out contritely, "I'll make this up to you by running Nadine's box over to the school this afternoon. Even better, I'll tie up these ribbons all pretty for ya."

Ruby shook her curly head with an exasperated smile. "It's impossible for your ma to stay mad at you. Did you know that, Buddy? It's just a plain impossible!"

## 6

$\longleftarrow$

By the time the bell at the grammar school rang to signal recess, Nadine was more than satisfied that Amy Jo had been absorbed into the second-grade mainstream. The altered dress had been blessedly accepted and Amy Jo had managed to intrigue the other children with her Midwestern twang and jump-rope skills. Despite Nadine's reluctance to throw Charmaine and Jake together the day before, she now had to admit the rewards made the risk worthwhile.

Nadine gazed out of one of the high windows overlooking the playground at the children frolicking over the parking lot and grassy yard. Resting her elbows on the faded sill, she wondered, not for the first time, what it would be like to have children of her own. Jake's babies.

With a sigh she propped her chin in her hand. How could she hope to entice him into that line of thinking without risking the relationship they already had? A noise inside the classroom startled her. She whirled to find Buddy Davis, of all people, loping into her classroom with a silver box tied in white ribbon tucked under his arm.

"Hey, Nadine," he drawled, raking his hand through

his loose thatch of hair as he scanned her curvy body, set to advantage in a pale green button-down dress.

Buddy? In school? She couldn't help gawking as she thought back to the times when they'd both been here as students. A few years ahead of her in the same class as Jake and Charmaine, he was constantly stomping down to the principal's office for one infraction or another—when he showed up for school at all.

"Buddy Davis!" another familiar voice snapped. "What did I just say to you not five minutes ago when you skulked by my office?"

Nadine had to bite back a laugh at the sight of Miss Brooks looming in the doorway, wearing the same outraged expression she'd worn back then.

Buddy lifted his hunched shoulders with a lopsided grin. "You were sayin' that your shoes were pinchin' you something fierce. That you were gonna change 'em before you went out with Farley Hendricks down to the butcher's."

Mildred Brooks's face whitened and her mouth thinned. "Not what you overheard, young man! What I told you, concerning your delivery to Miss Jordan during class time."

"Ain't class time, it's recess time," he puled.

Mildred Brooks raised a wagging finger. "Nevertheless, any courting—"

"Courting? Him? Me? Us?" Nadine's cries of dismay were drowned out by Buddy's own snort.

"I live too fast and loose for a schoolteacher," he objected bluntly, dropping the box on Nadine's desk. "This is a delivery from Ma's shop, that's all."

Nadine couldn't disguise her relief over the fact that the box was indeed from someone other than Buddy. Her features softened with hope as she made the most obvious deduction. Jake had presumably been to Buttons 'n' Bows this morning to return Amy Jo's clothes. This gift had to be from Jake. It just had to be.

"It's from Flynn, Nadine," Buddy confided, his demeanor bordering on humane. Perhaps he felt a kinship toward her in the face of their old taskmaster. "Came in this mornin'," he continued, "set on finding just the right present."

"Who? What is he talking about?" Mildred Brooks demanded tersely.

As Nadine groped for words, the bell ending recess rang inside and out with clarity.

"Get going, Buddy Davis," Mildred Brooks ordered, extending her thin arm toward the door with a sweeping motion.

"But I wanted to see her open—"

"Out. O-U-T, and I mean now!"

Buddy stayed put, shoving his hands in his jeans pockets with a belligerent stare. He eventually backed down, however, as children filing into the room began making faces at him and giggling over his slovenly appearance. Buddy was used as a bad example by many parents in town, who preached over and over again that if their children put a foot wrong in school, they'd "end up like that do-less boy Buddy Davis."

The bright new box resting on Nadine's open grade book immediately drew lots of attention. Even after the second bell rang to resume order, her students were clustering around her desk for a good close look. Mildred Brooks had clicked out briskly on Buddy's heels, no doubt intent on making sure he exited the building.

At the urging of the children, Nadine sank down in her chair and carefully undid the ribbon. She excitedly pried off the cover, took one look at the contents with a squeal and pushed the open box against her chest. Curious cries of protest from her students filled the air.

"Can't be a mouse," Petey Nudell decided with a shake of his tousled blond head. "She'd never put that up to her bosoms."

"The box is too skinny for any animal," the more practical Judy Lawson piped up with a flick of her brown braids.

Nadine could feel her heart thudding wildly beneath the thin cardboard, beneath the sexy red teddy she'd seen in Ruby's window for the past month. The only European import in town!

Despite this public exhibition and the sixteen innocent faces agog with interest, Jake's romantic intent sank in fast. He was courting her with wild, reckless extravagance.

"Hey, a card fell out," Amy Jo announced, pointing to the floor. "Want me to get it?"

"No!" Nadine promptly set her foot over the small white square that had fluttered down near her roomy book bag. "Time for everyone to get back to their desks," she announced briskly.

The group began to disperse with groans. Feeling she'd do well to offer some explanation to quell their curiosity, Nadine set the box in her top left drawer, folded the teddy into a small square, concealing the straps and lacy edging. When everyone was back in their seats, she held up the square. "See? It's a lovely new scarf."

The easily placated youngsters' groans turned to murmurs of awe.

"Put it on your head, Miz Jordan," Suzy Purvis called out, jumping to her feet at her second-row seat.

"Not right now," Nadine declined, feeling a blush

heating her cheeks as she returned the lingerie to the box. ''We have our art projects to finish.''

To her relief, the mere mention of their clay master-pieces sent the children diving into their desks for their work shirts. ''Now, who would like to explain all of this to Amy Jo?'' Several hands flew up and Nadine let them lead Amy Jo back to the cupboard to get a block of clay and show her their crude beginnings.

She waited until she was all but forgotten. Then ever so slowly, she reached down to capture the card hidden beneath her foot and set it in her lap. Her ivory hand trembled with anticipation as she gazed down to read the message.

> Wanted: dance lesson under
> the stars and tangled vines.
> Teach Me Tonight.
> Jake

Nadine read between the lines with a skittering pulse and wide green eyes. A secret rendezvous at the gazebo for a private *fais-dodo*? Surely that's what he was setting up, in a code that the nosy Ruby wouldn't have been able to crack. And he was giving her the option of not coming if she didn't have the same feelings for him. As if she'd miss it for the world!

Nadine moved in a daze the rest of the afternoon, but with superhuman effort managed to appear competent at school and businesslike as she ushered Amy Jo into Buttons 'n' Bows after school for another attempt at choosing her wardrobe.

Ruby acknowledged their arrival with a wave from a side counter that held knits, then turned her attention back to Celia Waters, a young mother with two toddlers tugging at her hands as she attempted to select a cardigan sweater.

Nadine steered Amy Jo to a rack holding some appropriate-looking children's items. She shifted her book tote from one shoulder to the other, again reminded of Jake's gift tucked away at the bottom of the large tan canvas sack. Out of sight, but hardly out of mind. As they'd passed by on the sidewalk just now, she'd noticed the gaping space in Ruby's window where the teddy had been displayed for so long. People were bound to notice the unusual lingerie's absence, but hopefully Ruby would keep her mouth shut. Gossip about even the sweetest romance could turn ugly if twisted by a vindictive person, and gossip about her romance with Jake could become fuel for the Parnells in their fight for their granddaughter.

Could this romance be any sweeter? Nadine couldn't see how. Jake was pulling out all the stops to declare himself. The extravagant purchase and the clandestine meeting, put to paper with a clever play on words...

He wanted her lessons to extend beyond his daughter, that was clear. Not that she was a femme fatale like Charmaine by any means. He would be her mentor in the mechanics of seduction. But she could teach him to love again, trust again, she decided with pride. That had to be the meaning of his message. He must understand that like his late wife, Nadine had the capacity to fulfill all his needs, provide a home for him and Amy Jo. Finally, she'd managed to outdo Charmaine in a manhunt!

Despite the thrill of victory, Nadine was having a bit of trouble accepting that she'd outdistanced her flirty, colorful sister so quickly. There seemed to be only one logical answer. Jake Flynn actually possessed the foresight and the insight to realize that it was the little sister who could provide the nurturing he and his daughter needed, a role that the self-centered Charmaine couldn't fill.

"Do you like this one?" Amy Jo peeped excitedly, pointing out a peach culotte dress.

Nadine smiled, emerging from her own thoughts. "It's right in style, Amy Jo. Would you like it in blue?" she suggested, taking one of the proper size off the rod for her. "Some of the girls already have the peach shade."

"Okay," the girl agreed, bobbing her dark head.

"And how about some of these oversized T-shirts?" Nadine asked, stepping over to an adjoining rack. "I believe that Ruby has some knit leggings to match them."

"I most surely do!" Ruby proclaimed. With a nod to the exiting Celia, she glided across the shop like a stocky ballroom dancer to assist them. "Right off, I want you to know that Jake took care of everything this morning. I have a credit slip all made out to Amy Jo over by the register. Though I'm heartbroken over some of the returns. And aghast at what you've done to that yellow dress she's wearing," she added with a pout.

"Now, Ruby," Nadine cut in, glancing toward Amy Jo. "The whole idea of Jake's coming here in advance was to avoid any dickering in front of the child."

"One of the reasons, anyhow," Ruby crowed softly, her round beady eyes aglow.

Ruby had to be teasing her about the teddy! Nadine cleared her throat in discomfort and leaned over to address the girl. "Why don't you take these things into the fitting room, honey. I'll be along in a minute. Oh, and take a couple pair of these shorts, too."

"Okay!" Amy Jo raced ahead to a small cubbyhole in the back and closed the white shuttered door behind her.

"It was thoughtful of Jake to think of me during his trip here today," Nadine went on to say, delighted to share the woman-to-woman confidence.

"Certainly was," Ruby agreed, reaching out to claw her chunky jeweled fingers through the bulging racks along with her customer. She had the nerve to hand Nadine something that Jake had returned only hours ago! Nadine handed it right back with an adamant shake of her strawberry-blond mane. "Perfect for ya," Ruby went on. "Jake's gift, I mean."

"You really think so?" Nadine queried brightly, amazed that anyone other than Jake had picked up on her more adventurous side.

"Lordy, yes," the older woman gushed. "Plain obvious what a flower like you needs."

"Did, uh, Jake choose it himself?" Nadine ventured to ask, her complexion pinkening.

"All his own doing," Ruby declared with traces of amazement. "Amazed at how well he knows women."

"Yes," Nadine agreed, joining Ruby in a girlish giggle. "You know, it's important that Jake seem the down-to-earth daddy, despite any purchases he's made here," she attempted to caution. "I mean, with Calder and Thelma Parnell after custody of Amy Jo..."

Ruby patted her dark curls, looking around to make sure the shop was still empty. "I realize he was trusting my discretion, especially over the touchier purchase. As he well should! I've always been fond of him."

"Jake can use all the support he can get," Nadine declared with a nod.

"Oh my, yes," Ruby oozed. "But I think you'll find

most folks plan to stay neutral. They accept the Parnells' uppity ways because of their wealth, because Calder has hired on several of them at the peanut farm. By the same token, they see Jake as a capable parent and know Will's home is a happy one.'' She leaned closer with a sober expression. ''If he's fixin' to marry soon, that of course will go over big with Judge Trimble at the custody hearing. And by his moves today...'' she trailed off wistfully.

Nadine couldn't help beaming in understanding. ''He might just have remarriage on his mind.''

''Such a bonus, too, having such a lovely sister-in-law waiting in the wings, eager to help out,'' Ruby unexpectedly added.

Bringing up Charmaine's part in things seemed odd to Nadine, but she let it pass. Instead, she forged on to protest Buddy's bold delivery to the school during class time.

''I never tell Buddy how to handle such things,'' Ruby explained haughtily, then added, ''It's just that Buddy so loves dropping over to say hello to Mildred Brooks. I understand that even after all these years she still remembers him vividly.'' Her cheeks bunched in a proud smile.

Nadine couldn't argue the fact, no matter how misinterpreted!

Amy Jo sang out for Nadine's assistance seconds later. Nadine wended her way through the cramped shop, aware that Ruby was following with more shirts.

They spent some time piecing together items that could be mixed and matched. After the final decisions had been made and Amy Jo was changing back into the altered dress, Ruby drew Nadine out of the small dressing room, and out of the child's earshot.

"Hate to tell you this, hon," Ruby said reluctantly, "but you don't have nearly enough credit to cover those things."

"But Jake returned two sacks full of clothing," Nadine whispered in sharp protest.

"Most of it was clearance," Ruby was forced to admit, looking down at the fat toes peeking out of her plastic sandals. "Styles from seasons past. Dollar for dollar, it was a whole lot cheaper than this new stock."

Nadine pulled her mouth tight. How ironic that Ruby was forced to admit to pushing old stuff. But the timing couldn't be worse. Amy Jo was expecting everything. Nadine had encouraged her to be extravagant. "Well, this puts me in a jam, Ruby," she hissed with a nervous glance at the shuttered door three feet away.

"Sor-ree," Ruby huffed, planting her hands on her ample hips.

Nadine inhaled, thinking hard and fast. She was fairly certain Jake was all tapped out, partly because of the gift he'd purchased for her. It seemed logical that she quietly take care of the deficit herself. But she'd settled with the milkman this morning on her way out the door and stopped in for her dry cleaning en route to class, which left her with about four dollars in her purse. She nibbled at her lower lip. "How much are we talking about, Ruby?"

"Thirty dollars would do it."

Nadine's forehead puckered in frustration. "I'm a bit short of that, I'm afraid."

Ruby frowned. "Well, surely after this fiasco, you can't expect me to extend extra credit, too!"

Nadine bit back her temper. "No, no, I wouldn't expect that of you, Ruby. You keep an eye on Amy Jo. I'll run home for the cash."

* * *

It took Nadine several minutes to scurry through the tree-lined streets, back to the Jordans' old gray two-story on Simpson. She made a beeline for the bright cozy kitchen and the ceramic spice jar that served as a bank for their household expense money. She dumped the contents on the counter and counted twenty-one dollars and twenty-seven cents in bills and coins. Adding that sum to the four in her wallet brought her close to the needed thirty. Maybe Charmaine could make up the difference, if she happened to be home.

Nadine charged up the staircase and into her big sister's mauve-and-mint bedroom. Her sensibilities always reeled upon impact with the bright and bold cabbage-figured wallpaper, the puffy chiffon curtains and the heavy pieces of pine furniture painted glossy white.

It could've been a haven for a female of any age, if it weren't for the curio cabinet chock-full of sensual aids, Charmaine's surefire potions for enticement and entrapment. She'd installed it bedside soon after the elder Jordans moved out. The first time Nadine had taken inventory of the scented candles, exotic oils, silken bonds and thick, sweet liqueurs, she'd naively asked Charmaine why there were no glasses for the drinks. Charmaine had erupted in mocking velvet laughter that had gone on forever, leaving little sister embarrassed about her sexual inexperience.

There would be no sparring today, Nadine realized gratefully as she caught sight of Charmaine seated at her dressing table in her slip, primping before a round makeup mirror. Big sister obviously had other concerns. Her outfit, a navy scooped-neck dress dotted with stars, was tossed carelessly on her frilly lilac bedspread, and her white sandals were discarded on the hardwood flooring. It appeared that for some reason, Charmaine had rushed in, stripped quickly, then plopped down to study her own reflection.

"I need to borrow five dollars," Nadine announced abruptly.

"I can't think of money at a time like this," Charmaine lamented, shifting on the stool.

Nadine peered over Charmaine's shoulder as the distressed blonde pressed her manicured fingers gently into her cheeks. "You got any money up here?" she asked.

"Tell me true, Nadine," her sister demanded breathlessly. "Am I losing my looks?"

"Losing…" Nadine trailed off in a hoot of disbelief. "Of course not!"

Charmaine's pouty lips immediately curved. "I didn't think so. I've been sitting here for over an hour, wondering…"

An hour wasted away when she could've been making them a chicken salad for supper? Nadine worked to conceal her annoyance. "You look divine. Now about that five…"

Charmaine expelled a deep breath that lifted her wispy bangs. "It just has to be him, then. He doesn't understand that I'm all revved up and waiting."

Nadine froze. Him? Charmaine had to be talking about Jake. Obviously, something had tipped Charmaine off to the fact that he might not be ready to leap into her silken web. Did she already know about Nadine receiving the teddy? That would be a disaster! Charmaine would uncork every bottle in her curio to fight back. And Nadine was no match for her expertise.

"What's the matter?" Nadine asked, praying her voice didn't betray her anxiety.

"Oh, Jake sent me a gift through Ruby," Charmaine

sputtered, lifting a fashion magazine off a silver box identical to the one Nadine had received except for the different color ribbon.

Nadine ducked as the oversized journal came flying over her sister's bare shoulder and landed on the hardwood floor with a resounding slap. Nadine suddenly felt like she'd been slapped, hard, across the face. Was Jake toying with them? Supplying them both with provocative lingerie to promote open rivalry? She told herself not to jump to conclusions. The first step was to find out what was beneath the rainbow assortment of handkerchiefs heaped on the box.

"So what's the big surprise?" Nadine asked, forcing a steady tone and a smile. "Under these pastel hankies, I mean."

"That's just the trouble," Charmaine wailed. "Nothing! Nothing but more handkerchiefs!" She tossed them in the air one by one in a childish fit, sending them sailing through the air like dainty lace-edged parachutes.

"Really?" Nadine's voice reflected wonder. So Jake was making a clear choice as an honest man should. And she was the one! But she would keep it a secret until they'd made love. Crossing that intimate line was the only way to prove to Charmaine that Jake was settled in his commitment.

Charmaine's soft brows furrowed over her small perfect nose. "Have you ever heard of anything so provincial?"

"That's Cherry Creek for you, though," Nadine argued evenly as she stooped to retrieve the hankies. "It's part of our local charm, being downright provincial. Jake knows that as well as anybody."

"He would have to start out carefully, I suppose," Charmaine said, somewhat mollified. She reached for the small enclosure card and held it up for study, making it easy for Nadine to catch a glimpse of the message.

> With sincere appreciation
> for all you do.
> Jake

Nadine's creamy forehead creased slightly as she mulled over the note. It seemed odd—Charmaine wasn't often recognized for her charitable ways. Then she shrugged off her lingering doubts and decided to just accept things as they were. She was the winner! And Charmaine would survive. She flitted through flings like a honeybee moving from flower to flower.

Charmaine dropped the card into her jewelry box with a click of her tongue. "Snagging Jake is going to take more patience than I figured, I guess."

"Maybe you should just give up," Nadine suggested quietly.

"Give up?" Charmaine parroted. She swiveled her bottom on the stool to face her sister. "There isn't another promising man for miles around!" She turned back to the mirror and picked up her brush. "I've scoured this town. You know how I've scoured this town."

Nadine rolled her eyes. Charmaine sure didn't sound desperately in love, just plain desperate! It justified Nadine's subterfuge all the more. She loved Jake with all her heart and soul. She would cherish him, choose him out of a lineup of a thousand men. "Listen, Charmaine, I don't have time to discuss this now," she claimed hurriedly. "I was just over at Ruby's, redoing Amy Jo's wardrobe, and I fell short of cash."

Charmaine shook her brush at her. "I should be livid over the way you handled those clothes."

Nadine swallowed a grin. Wait until Charmaine found out what else she was going to handle! "Amy Jo is waiting. Can you spare the five dollars or not?"

"Oh, all right!" Charmaine snapped in surrender. "Boy, that Ruby can be a pirate with her merchandise." She yanked open the bottom drawer of her dressing table and extracted a bill from a neat little roll. "Here. Go live it up!"

Nadine gave her sister's hair a tug. "You're a prize!"

Charmaine rolled her eyes. "To some more than others, it seems."

Nadine crossed the floor but paused in the doorway when Charmaine called out. "What is it, Charmaine?" she asked on a sigh.

"This might be stretching it a bit, but maybe Jake gave me those handkerchiefs with the notion that you might sew me up another rainbow-colored *fais-dodo* costume."

Nadine threw her arms in the air with a shrill cry of disgust. "With six tiny handkerchiefs? They wouldn't begin to cover anything!"

"So what do you think, Nadine?" she called out as Nadine stormed down the stairs. "Yes or no?"

Things were no calmer back at Buttons 'n' Bows, Nadine soon discovered. She flew back inside the shop to find Thelma Parnell standing at the central counter beside a beaming Amy Jo. Nadine's heart wrenched at the resemblance between the two. It was evident that they shared the same high cheekbones, blue eyes and high forehead. It seemed so right that Thelma be a part of her grandchild's life, but so wrong that she wanted to run it completely.

"Why, Nadine, I was beginning to wonder if you got

lost,'' Ruby tittered edgily, lifting her chubby shoulders in a gesture of helplessness behind Thelma.

"Hello, Thelma," Nadine greeted breathlessly. "I just had to step out for a few minutes."

"I know why you left," Thelma returned. She was brisk in manner, as usual, but humming with a new kind of happiness, too.

Nadine studied her nervously. "What do you mean?"

Thelma sighed impatiently, closing her boxy gold-clasped purse with a distinctive click, as though securing Fort Knox. "Dollars and cents, of course. The bottom line always."

"I was just doing some tabulating when Thelma showed up," Ruby intervened, patting her curls. "Naturally, she wondered why her grandchild was alone. I simply told her that you were a little short of funds and—"

"And Grandma helped," Amy Jo inserted excitedly, bouncing in her tennis shoes. "Even bought me more things."

Thelma's austerely set features softened in the radiance of Amy Jo's smile.

Amy Jo squeezed Thelma's veined hand. "She's wonderful."

Nadine released a harried breath as she absorbed the unexpected glitch.

Thelma measured the schoolteacher's situation accurately. "I imagine you went digging into a nest egg to make up the difference, dear. That is entirely unnecessary now. As a matter of fact, I'd be honored to buy you a new spring outfit, as well—"

"No, Thelma," Nadine gasped with raised palms. "I am perfectly capable of paying my way."

"Well, Calder and I are thrilled that you liked the

roses,'' she added craftily. ''As close as you are to the Flynns, you've always been dear to the Parnells, too.''

''Yes,'' Nadine said, struggling for safe ground between appreciation and rejection.

''We loved the roses, Grandma,'' Amy Jo piped up.

Thelma gave the child's head a gentle pat. ''You shall have some of your very own, dear. Fresh ones in your room at Grandma's house.''

Amy Jo's shiny eyes looked up at Thelma. ''Whenever I come to visit?''

Thelma's red mouth tugged smugly. ''You won't ever need for a thing once you're settled with Grandpa Calder and me,'' she promised.

Nadine braced herself against a shelf of summer gloves. Had she been away minutes or hours? Somehow, during her short absence, Thelma had managed to ingratiate herself with the child and tempt her with the promise of better things on the family farm. Thelma's yearnings were, of course, more than understandable. What mother didn't want to know her children's children? And what young girl didn't dream of a doting grandmother? The mutual need between Thelma and Amy Jo had no doubt hurried the bonding process along.

Nadine twisted the strap of her purse into a huge knot. Jake was going to be furious with her for allowing this to happen.

''I better be on my way,'' Thelma announced, turning her thin wrist to read the face of her gold watch. ''I was on my way to the cleaners when I spotted my angel in here.'' She dropped a kiss on Amy Jo's forehead and marched out with a regal wave.

Nadine stepped up to the counter and took hold of the two bulging pink sacks with frustrated noises.

''Hey, don't give me the evil eye,'' Ruby complained,

pounding the glass countertop. "Ain't my fault she came flying in here like the Queen Mother herself."

Nadine's glare didn't waver. Ruby was eating up the drama like a box of tasty bonbons. "Where do we stand, creditwise, Ruby?"

"Hell, Jake's got all his original credit," Ruby reported. "Thelma paid for all the child's new clothes."

"Oh, no!" Nadine whirled back toward the entrance, hoping for a glimpse of Thelma, even though she knew the woman was long gone.

"Didn't want me to even mention it to you," Ruby leaned over the counter to confide. "I wouldn't go tell Jake if I were you. The boy seems on the ropes as it is."

How could he help it, with all the pressure he was facing? Nadine silently mused. She understood Thelma's game, too. She'd bring up the huge purchase at the hearing. Nadine winced as her heart squeezed painfully. The way things were going, Jake was more likely to strangle her than make love to her!

"That purse of yours is lookin' mighty beaten," Ruby noted, gesturing to the knot in the strap. "Why not enjoy some of that credit yourself?"

"Oh, shut up, Ruby!" With one hand locked on the bags and the other on Amy Jo's arm, Nadine flew out of the shop like a hurricane.

# 7

"Hello, Charmaine." Jake's voice was liquid sensuality later that evening as he edged past his father and set the old black telephone of his youth on the kitchen table. Wishing for some privacy, he tipped his raven head to direct Will from the room. Will merely rolled his eyes and continued to dry the dishes at the sink. Jake sank down in a padded chrome chair with a sigh and stretched his long muscular legs. "You get my gift? Mmm, that's good."

A burning frisson chased up his spine as he once again envisioned Charmaine in the tiny red teddy. If only his nosy old father would give him some space for a little sweet talk. He frowned again at Will, who continued to dry silverware with deliberate precision, setting each piece in the drawer as though handling sterilized surgical instruments.

"It seemed so you, Sassy," he murmured, above the rhythmic clink of the cutlery. "Sure I mean it, honey," he said, perplexed by her angry tone. "Thought it was just the feminine thing. Is the size wrong?" he ventured to ask. "Seemed smaller than ones I've seen, but I figured the lacy edges would make up for it."

The chrome chair squeaked as he turned away from Will, cupping the mouthpiece closer to his mouth. "You get the card, too? Wonderful,'' he crooned. ''Nice night, isn't it? Warm for hours yet, I bet.'' He started as Will clanged a frying pan and a pot together before storing them in the cupboard beside the stove. ''Do I what?'' he asked, his heavy brows jumping to his hairline. ''No, I don't think you should sew the lacy edges together, Charmaine. It would spòil the fun... Well, sure, if you really have to shampoo your hair. See you soon though,'' he said significantly. ''Bye.''

''Somebody a little out of sorts?'' Will queried, snapping his son's solid shoulder with the tip of his towel.

Jake jammed the receiver back in its cradle. ''I'm fine!''

''I meant Charmaine,'' his father corrected.

''Have you ever felt on solid ground with that one, Dad?''

''Never felt completely safe with either one,'' the older man confessed, rubbing his white whiskers.

Jake rose from the table to put the phone in its usual place on the counter near the Winnie-the-Pooh cookie jar. ''You keep trying to caution me about how interchangeable the sisters are,'' he complained. ''I've had enough of your innuendos.''

Will reared back his silvered head. ''Innuendos? I thought I was being crystal clear.''

Jake lifted Pooh's head off to snag a couple of fresh, soft macaroons. How could he come down too hard on a father who'd baked his afternoon away? ''If a man could find the best in a woman,'' he theorized thoughtfully, ''it would be a blend of the sexy Charmaine and the endearing Nadine.''

''Can't argue that point,'' Will answered, sinking into the chair his son had just vacated. ''I hope you'd be smart enough to snatch her up if you come across her.''

Jake leaned into the counter, munching on a coconut wafer. "I think that Amy Jo and I are better off as a twosome. I wouldn't dream of putting her through another ordeal like we had with Rosemary."

"I doubt you'd lose a second wife to cancer," Will objected mildly.

"No, but I might divorce!" his son shot back. "And a loss is a loss."

"Won't lose your woman to divorce if you keep things right under your roof," Will argued with fraying patience.

"I just feel like the girl and I finally got our life back on track," Jake went on to explain. "Like we were in a long dark tunnel and we're blinking in the light again!"

"Some dynamic duo! You haven't hardly been able to move a muscle without the help of those next door," Will declared bluntly.

"Thanks a lot, Dad!" Jake threw his hands in the air. "Why not go all the way and support the Parnells?" he added snidely.

Will sighed patiently. "All I'm saying, son, is that you can't expect to do it alone! And it's a sad thing not to have a wife in your house."

"The Jordans are only a house away," Jake argued. "And seem more than happy with the arrangement so far."

Will gave him a skeptical look. "You ask 'em?"

"Well, no," Jake admitted slowly. As he sauntered over to take a chair beside his father, he thought about Nadine's luminous look when she'd arrived for Amy Jo's tutoring earlier in the evening and Charmaine's cranky tone on the phone just now. He was feeling less confident. But he was sure if he kept at it, his plan would succeed. They both still liked him a lot. He was sure of that. And what harm could come from having some good times? "They're both quite outspoken," he maintained. "I'm sure if one has a complaint, she'll share it."

Will stared at him with unblinking incredulity. "I've never known women to be that direct in matters of love. Usually things surface at unexpected times, in unexpected ways. And is the man ready? Nosiree, he is not!"

Jake inhaled impatiently. "What are you telling me, Dad?"

"Nothing new, son. Only that this scheme of yours is doomed by the very laws of nature. Man has had woman trouble since the dawn of time. Just as sisters have sparred with one another since the dawn of time." He rubbed his chin. "None of that is about to fall into place just for you! Sure, you've had your pain," he granted, "but women are forever plotting and planning and dreaming of their one and only true love. They expect commitment. They expect exclusivity. They expect a man to make a choice."

"I haven't caught a whiff of orange blossoms yet," Jake argued.

"But if you do, you'll immediately spout off about your plans to remain a bachelor father?" Will challenged.

Jake swallowed hard. "Well, sure I will. But I tell you, I know them both like the back of my hand, and there's not going to be trouble."

Will reached across the table and traced a finger across his son's open palm, studying it intently. "Then one of these lines must spell Dumbo."

Jake snatched his hand away with a betrayed glare. "I wish you'd let me handle my own affairs, Dad."

Will looked off into space, drumming his fingers on

the table. "Just remember there's a lot of sensitive issues at stake. That there's a price even for play."

"Not if both parties agree on the rules of the game," Jake objected sharply. "If they understand that true love's not involved."

Will jabbed a finger at his son. "Serve you right to fall in love again," he snorted.

"That won't happen unless I make it happen," Jake stated loftily, hoping his lower lip wasn't visibly trembling. He was as nervous and anxious as a kid wondering if Charmaine would show up out back tonight. If she didn't come, he'd understand that his offer wasn't enough. That like Nadine, she expected a vine-covered cottage and a band of gold. Damn Will for making him think so much!

"Best of luck to you, Dumbo!" Will crowed.

Jake was about to raise further argument when the swinging door to the dining room bounced open and Nadine entered the kitchen with a book and tablet tucked in the crook of her arm. Jake swallowed and rubbed away the frown on his face.

"All finished for the night," she announced brightly, her eyes shifting from one male to the other. "Did I interrupt something?"

"Not at all," Will assured her jovially. "So how did the first tutoring session go?"

"Amy Jo and I went over the finer points of geography this round," she reported, tapping her book.

"She catching on?" Jake asked anxiously, his pending rendezvous with Charmaine temporarily evaporating from his thoughts.

"Yes," Nadine answered. "Of course this crash course is designed only to raise her test scores for Saturday's hearing. Once we get the custody nonsense out of the way, we'll have the summer for real catch-up and review.''

Will pulled out a chair for her. ''She being a good sport?''

Nadine sank across from Jake with a faint smile. ''I want to speak to you about that.''

Jake leaned over and grasped her hand. ''What's wrong?''

Nadine wrinkled her nose over his earnestness. ''Nothing! It's just that she doesn't understand why she has to work so hard this week.''

Will folded his white cotton towel in a neat rectangle and hung it on the oven handle. ''She would wonder, not knowing about the custody battle.''

''I took the liberty of telling her that these tests were yearly finals for the school records—which is true—and that if she buckles down this week in particular, you'd treat her to the carnival on the weekend.''

''Oh, with the hearing and all, I wasn't planning to go to the carnival!'' Jake protested. ''It comes every year. There'll be other times.''

Nadine sighed hard. ''Jake, I promised. If you don't want to go, I'll take her myself.''

''We'll all go,'' Will interceded. ''That'll show the Parnells and Judge Trimble and the whole town just how happy we are!''

Jake heaved a breath, his scowl softening. ''I know when I'm licked.''

''Hell, just say you're wrong when you're wrong.'' Will grinned.

Jake laughed. ''Okay, Dad, I was wrong.'' He gazed intently at Nadine, his mouth curving warmly. ''Won't hurt any of us to have some fun.''

Nadine's pulse sprang to life. Surely he wasn't referring to the carnival now, not when they were set to meet in the gazebo in a matter of hours! Oh, how she longed to be alone with him, feel his hands all over her, hear his hot little whispers. Finally, she'd have him all to herself, and it was all his idea!

What was going on in her pretty little head? Jake wondered, blinking several times to see if he was imagining the disturbing gleam in her eyes. But the green sparkle remained hypnotically steady, joining the two of them in a long electric moment. It wasn't any real mystery, though, he ultimately decided. Nobody loved the traveling carnival with its Ferris wheel and cotton candy more than Nadine. He should've remembered that.

Nadine rose to leave a short while later, declining Will's offers of cookies and drinks. Jake stood up, too, and moved to the fridge for a beer. "Oh, yeah," he said as she reached the back screen door. "Thanks for dealing with Ruby this afternoon. With any luck this will be the end of Buttons 'n' Bows for a while."

Nadine pinkened guiltily under his grateful look. Obviously, Amy Jo hadn't mentioned that Thelma had picked up the tab for all those clothes. She waged a brief inner tug-of-war over duty versus pleasure. Should she immediately tell him the unhappy fact, or conceal it to keep their sexual encounter lighthearted? In the end, she decided it was her duty to give Jake pleasure tonight, and nothing more.

Fresh out of the shower after midnight, dressed only in gray sweatpants, Jake began to watch the gazebo. Luckily, his bedroom faced the backyard, so he had a bird's-eye view of the rendezvous point he'd suggested.

So he sat on the window frame, with his broad bare back braced against the old varnished wood, one knee drawn up beneath his chin, exhaling smoke from one of the few cigarettes he allowed himself each week. The night was indigo velvet, with just enough moonlight to give the trees and shrubs intriguing shadow and substance. Jake knew he could be seen from the hedge dividing the Flynns' back lawn from the Jordans'. If Charmaine made the effort to come halfway, she'd see the glow of his cigarette.

Would she come? Up until her briskness on the phone tonight, she'd had all the symptoms of a woman on the make. What had caused the change? He went over the entire weekend, from her pointing out the sexy teddy in the window display to their Sunday afternoon tour around town. They'd met up with some old high school friends, who in turn had organized a casual reunion at the diner. Charmaine had been a cuddly temptress all the while, leaning against him, pinching his rear, tweaking his cheek, openly and publicly staking her claim on him. He hadn't minded. It felt good to be desired for a change. As long as it was in good fun, like he'd told Will.

Just as he was beginning to fear that he was going to puff away his weekly quota of smokes in one sitting, he heard a rustle of movement next door. His gaze darted to the hedge searching for any movement. Sure enough, he spotted a splash of red and a banner of gold edging through the break between the dense foliage and the front fence. He sat still for a couple more puffs to make certain he was noticed, then stubbed out his butt, eased himself off the sill and stealthily made his way through the house.

Nadine's heart was pumping like a tiny jackhammer as she scampered into the Flynns' backyard with deep, gulping breaths. The soft grass was cool on the soles of her tender feet, and her limbs tingled with tiny scratches from her scramble through the hedge.

She felt all arms and legs as she almost tumbled forward. There was a deliciously disturbing core of fire centered between her thighs, a throbbing, hollow place yearning to be filled. She'd felt the same rush on occasions in the past over a sexy thought, or in the throes of a lusty kiss. But the promise of ultimate fulfillment, with the man she'd loved since grammar school, left her in a trembling haze of heat.

She gracefully ducked inside the Flynns' green-roofed gazebo, a hand on the column of her throat as she caught her breath. Aside from Jake, seated in his upstairs window, she didn't want to be spotted by anyone. She felt quite safe now within the white wooden pentagon, covered in flowery clematis vines. She sagged into a corner, breathing quick shallow breaths. He was on his way right now. By the time she'd reached the Flynns' biggest pecan tree midway between the hedge and house, Jake's shadowy form had vanished from the window.

Feeling just a bit uncomfortable in the snug-fitting teddy, Nadine moved to the center of the gazebo and bent over to stretch the fabric and her stiff limbs.

Jake slipped into the garden house then, just in time to catch the sight from a side angle—an untamed beauty, bowed at the waist, caught in her own personal moment, her face lost in a tide of shimmery hair. Slender beams of white light filtered through the latticework, giving the vision a necromantic quality.

Was she aware of him yet? Was her pose staged? With Charmaine, one never knew where the games began or ended. Eager to play along in any case, he prowled closer with the stealth of a panther, covertly watching as her fingers pulled and tugged the teddy down her torso.

The shiny red silk straining across the curve of rounded bottom reminded him of a sweet maraschino cherry. His shaft went rigid in his loose knit pants as he longed to enter her, own her, just for a little while.

"Sassy..." The name erupted from his throat in a muffled moan.

As Nadine straightened her spine, her mane fell away from her features in a golden-red shower. "I can't tell you how long I've waited to hear you call me that, darling," she whispered breathlessly.

"But..." Jake's mouth went dry as he tried to speak. Just as well, since he didn't know what on earth to say anyway. It had to be a mistake. Little Nadine? Poised in panting longing? He blinked again and again, each time sure he'd find Charmaine in her place. But no, it was still the pert young schoolteacher, drilling him with a look of emerald intent, poised to pounce on his body like an anxious sex kitten.

His gaze roved her length, looking for a safe place to light. There was none. Her eyes gleamed captivatingly. Her mouth curved in a sultry pucker. Her breasts poured out of two minuscule lace pockets like thick whipped cream. The cradle of her hips flared invitingly, rocking gently to a silent rhythm inside her.

She was dynamite from head to toe. Sizzling, explosive, sexy.

He inhaled slowly, lowering his lids to block out her intoxicating image. She was obviously here because she wanted to be here. But it was all a mistake! This was the wrong sister for a friendly no-strings fling. Nadine wasn't the type to settle for half a relationship, half a heart, half an anything! Was she?

Hadn't his own father cautioned him about the Jordan girls being interchangeable after dark? It seemed the wily old man had been right! Jake felt like a bumbling fool to have doubted all the mating signs that Nadine had sent him in her own astute way: asking him what he wanted for himself, intervening when Charmaine had steered him onto the Jordan's porch swing, never resisting the opportunity for closeness.

"You look dumbstruck," Nadine crooned, oozing against him with a liquid motion.

He shivered as her soft arms skimmed the sides of his neck and her silky body rubbed into his. "I am, honey," he confessed hoarsely, running his fingers along her hourglass waistline. "I never expected it to be...quite like this."

"How clever of you to tune into my desires," she confided, smiling into his shadowed features. "How wonderful of you to take action so swiftly."

He shook his head; raven hair fell across his forehead. "I simply can't believe you want me—this much, I mean," he said dazedly. "It's like a dream."

She pressed closer, fingering a lock of hair above his brow. "The teddy and the note were my dream come true. My lifelong dream."

He sucked air through his teeth as he strained to think. How careless of Ruby to confuse the boxes! She'd probably been so excited about unloading the exorbitantly priced lingerie she hadn't been thinking clearly. But it would do no good to blame the busybody for her mistake. Everything was turned upside down, and that was that.

It wasn't much comfort, but his telephone conversation with Charmaine now made sense. After pointing out the teddy in Buttons 'n' Bows, she'd gotten the harmless hankies instead, along with an innocuous note that reflected respect rather than amorous intent. No wonder she'd spoken of sewing lace edges together. She was expecting something sexy to wear!

And that was only half the incredible story. Nadine received the sensual gift and was thrilled, and had apparently not questioned the fact that it was meant for her. His ego told him that he could've done well with two teddies, but common sense rejoined that he wouldn't have lived long enough to enjoy it!

A coyness curved her lips as her fingers roamed his bare shoulders. "You seem lost for words."

"Honey, I can barely breath," he croaked.

"Aren't really here for talkin' anyway, are we?" She stood up on tiptoe, nuzzling her face into his matted chest.

His pulse leapt to life in panic and desire as her tongue grazed his skin and her teeth nipped at his nipple. A man was supposed to say no to this? Declare it a misunderstanding?

He was about to do just that. Then she made a crazy sound. An ardent moan as heavy as the humid night air. He blanked out entirely, rock hard and in flames. Unmasking this controlled, proper lady to find a wild, hot seductress was unbelievably erotic. She had depth, all right. Layers and layers of hidden emotion were suddenly surfacing in a dizzying spiral. Her face belonged to someone else with its gleaming gaze and parted mouth, belonged to a demanding, insatiable lover who would settle for nothing but total satisfaction. Her hands were all over him, claiming, exploring with bold strokes. Her moan soon lowered to a purr of approval.

"I thought— I thought—" He tried to tell her again, then realized that the longing to do so was gone. Suddenly Charmaine's charms seemed indescribably obvious in comparison. And it wasn't Char's fault at all. There was just no rival for this irresistible new Nadine!

"I thought I would die in your kitchen tonight," she confessed huskily. "Acting so proper for Will's sake, when all I wanted to do was reach out and touch you all over."

Jake inhaled dizzily as her fingernails scratched the breadth of his back, sinking just deep enough to make his skin tingle. No wonder she had been beaming like a hungry cat back in the kitchen! She was looking ahead to this! How naive of him to imagine she was thinking of the carnival!

"Your note was sweet," she purred on. "But we both know who's going to teach whom, don't we?"

"We do?" he rasped in genuine confusion. He hadn't been right about much so far and wasn't about to hazard a guess on that loaded question.

She drew him into a secret world for two, cocooned him with her soft laughter and inviting expression. "You're the one who's going to teach me tonight, Jake. Despite your message, I'm here to learn."

"Oh, Nadine…" He groaned, slumping back on the wall. "I never meant to—"

She closed right in on him. "You can't be having regrets already. You've barely touched me."

His expression ached. "I know it. Don't you think I know it?"

With a laugh she fell against his off-kilter form, pushing their weight into the latticework. She mistook his hesitant grunt for structural concern. "Don't worry. Will made these walls sturdy, to last a good long time. No matter what, they're not going to come tumbling down."

He swallowed hard and found his throat nearly closed. She didn't expect simple sex. She expected rambunctious abandon! The kind of mating he'd have had with Charmaine.

Nadine adjusted her body until it was flush with his, then moved her flat little belly over his shaft, testing its rigidity with gentle pressure and a croon of approval.

Jake's fingertips and hips caught the ledge behind him just when he thought he'd melt away like butter in the sun. Little Nadine Jordan was actually seducing him. And his body was playing traitor to his common sense, responding to her overtures like a tautly strung guitar aching to be plucked. Jake closed his eyes, surrendering to the glorious sensations bringing every inch of him to life.

If she sensed his uncertainty, it didn't slow her up. Her touch was everywhere—on his jaw, his throat, his chest. Then, finally, her fingers skimmed over the top of his knit pants and cupped his rigid flesh through the fabric of his pants. Several squeezes left him on the brink of explosion.

"Nadine..." His called her name in raspy reverence. "Do you understand what you're doing? To us? To me?"

"It's what we both have been longing for, darling. Why would you start to worrying now?"

A galvanic force filled his rib cage as she handled him again with more pressure, sending liquid lightning through his veins. Whatever her intentions, whatever the misunderstanding with the lingerie, he was going to take her. He couldn't help himself.

Nadine cried out in delight when Jake clamped his hands on her silky red bottom and kneaded her solid flesh with strong fingers. She rested her head on his collarbone, molding herself into the hardened male planes beneath her, all the while languishing in his massaging hands. She slowly lifted her head to study him with a look of unmistakable affection.

How had he missed this feline side of her? he wondered in a haze of masculine pride and need. If anything, her hunger was deeper than his own. It suddenly seemed the most natural thing in the world to dip down and capture her lips with his.

Nadine's mouth reminded him of newly cut sugar-cane—fresh, sweet and delicious. She gasped slightly as his tongue moved between her lips, then grazed the tender lining of her cheeks. Encouraged, his hands traveled up her back and around to her breasts and gave them a gentle squeeze. Her nipples hardened to solid brown points against their lacy barriers. Jake dipped his head to draw one, then the other, into his mouth, fabric and all. The friction of the lace and the salty taste of her skin sent his system reeling.

He was mildly aware of her lifting his hips and tugging at his pants, then abruptly startled when his bottom hit the cool white enameled ledge with a bare slap of skin. With elfin grace and mischief, she climbed up into his lap and wrapped her smooth thighs around his sinewy, hair-roughened ones.

Jake shuddered as her silken-covered crotch bore down on his solid manhood. Longing for more exquisite contact, he grasped the undercurve of bottom and glided her back and forth over his rigid flesh.

"This can't be you, Nadine," he rasped in helpless wonder.

"You make me wanton," she whispered earnestly. "Jake Flynn, you make me long for all sorts of insane things."

"And you make me want to give them to you, honey." He knew he could satisfy her, if that's what she truly desired. And he could more than satisfy himself. His fingers invaded the lace edging her hips, tentatively at first, before boldly plunging into the moist folds of her intimate opening.

Nadine gasped in wonder. It was the first time a man had ever done such a thing to her. The fact that it was Jake, the love of her life, made it all the more special, worth the wait.

Jake stroked and teased her for a time, swiftly drawing her into a heightened awareness she never knew existed. When he finally released the two bottom snaps holding the teddy together, she was on the brink of shattering in her own private heaven.

In his own way, Jake, too, was a goner. His eyes were glazed with passion, his nostrils musty with her scent. Without a single beat of hesitation, he drew her over his shaft and entered her, shuddering to the depths of his soul over the snug fit. He moved in slow, gentle thrusts, gradually coming to realize that she was tight in an untouched way. But how could it be, after this bold come-on? He worried, fleetingly, about just how much this had to mean to her, before he burrowed deep inside her to indulge his senses.

They shuddered together in a perspiring heap in a short while, and Jake cradled her in his arms as their passions ebbed away. Floating in a cloud of sated exhaustion, he barely noticed that he was still leaning awkwardly into the wooden ledge with Nadine astraddle, her legs limp against his thighs. Not prepared to face her, he kept her head against his chest, gently stroking her rich mane of hair. He suspected that when she did meet his gaze, she'd be the steady Nadine he'd always known, the level-headed Nadine who, in a saner state of mind, would never have behaved this way. Would she condemn him? After all, her virginity was gone in a matter of a few driving seconds. He deserved most of the blame. He was older, experienced, the teacher by her own admission. Being pathetically needy was his best excuse, his only excuse. Not very gallant.

Jake felt a resurgence of his own common sense, as though hit head-on by a cold bucket of water. He had to reach an understanding with this unpredictable charmer, find out what she wanted of him. For his sake, her sake, and the sake of his daughter. So much was riding on her support of Amy Jo. With effort, he captured her chin in his hand and looked into her eyes. "You all right?"

She nodded, blinking her sensuous heavy lids. As predicted, the sweet charm that had defined her for a lifetime was already seeping back into her features. Her smile actually held a shyness, a modesty that belied their intimate position.

"When you said you wanted me to teach you, honey, I didn't—I didn't realize..."

"That I was a virgin?" she finished huskily.

"Yes."

"That's perfectly all right, Jake," she murmured, bracing her hands on his chest. "You were perfectly wonderful. Everything I dreamed you'd be."

He released a tremendous sigh that visibly lifted his broad chest. "Then we're all right."

"Of course we are!" she answered softly. A comfortable pause followed before she asked, "So how long have you known?"

He twirled some of her gleaming hair around his finger, avoiding her gaze. "Known what?"

"That I'm madly in love with you, of course," she crooned in mild reproof, gently swiping her hand across his whiskered cheek. "Did you know it the minute you walked into my classroom, darling? Did you know it then?"

Terror stricken, he shook his head with force. "No, I didn't know it then!" Just as he hadn't known it a minute ago. A millisecond ago! Love? She loved him? Somehow he'd just dipped lower than pathetic. He'd taken a woman's virginity not realizing that she was in love with him! "Nadine, Nadine," he sought to explain. "Men aren't always as insightful about such things."

"I've been trying not to push you," she claimed. Her lush lower lip extended in a pout that looked a little too much like her sister's.

He was the first to admit that his flaming libido hadn't needed more than a tap in the right direction. But that admission would only insult her more than his calling her pushy! He understood that much about women.

"Please call me Sassy again, Jake," she wheedled with sparkling eyes. "And we can do this one more time if you want to."

Jake gingerly eased her off his lap with a dry, weary chuckle and swiftly pulled his pants back into place. "I couldn't possibly do it all over again—Sassy." He added the tag haltingly, feeling a rush of guilt over the fact that his wolfish greeting had always been exclusively reserved for Charmaine.

"That's fine," she said agreeably, adjusting her lingerie. "It is late, and a school night." She stood on tiptoe and kissed his nose. "Sweet dreams."

Jake watched her turn to leave. Everything was happening so swiftly—at her bidding! He clenched his fists, feeling a little like a puppet. "We need to talk," he called restlessly, trailing after her. "About this. About us. About everybody!"

She laughed softly, pausing on the gazebo's single white plank step. "It'll all keep until after the custody hearing, darling. Until you have Amy Jo free and clear, we'll play the teacher-parent charade for all to see. And don't you worry about Ruby spilling the beans about this teddy, either. We had a talk about discretion, and you can count on her to keep quiet."

Jake grimaced, rubbing his hands over his face. What a farce of a talk that must have been, Ruby assuming that Nadine got the handkerchiefs!

"Just as long as we have our own understanding, Jake," she continued passionately, "no one can destroy the burning bond between us."

What! He couldn't afford another round of burning bonding! How dare she assume it was so? Jake absorbed her parting shocker as she scampered back across the lawn. He should pursue her, corner her at the hedge, correct her assumption, chastise her for being so foolish and irresistible. But he couldn't take the risk of offending her at this crucial crossroad in his life. Why, she might turn on him in favor of the Parnells.

Jake ran a hand through his disheveled hair. No, Nadine wasn't capable of such a cruel turnabout. Not under ordinary circumstances, anyway. But she wasn't just any woman scorned; she was a woman who gave up her virginity on the faith of that precious four-letter word.

He slowly wandered back toward the house in a daze, thinking about the very thing he was so anxious to steer clear of: love.

# 8

"To think that all these years I figured Buddy Davis to be the dumbest boy this town ever grew!" Will topped off the remark with a snort as he paced round his garage the following morning.

Jake was standing at his father's workbench, slowly stirring a can of canary-yellow house paint. "We'd all be better off if you weren't such a restless sleeper, Dad."

Will's bushy white brows narrowed as Jake turned to confront him. "Meaning you wouldn't have confided in me if I hadn't caught sight of Nadine flitting back home last night."

"Well, let's say I wish you had skipped that trip to the kitchen to heat up a glass of milk," Jake answered, turning back to his paint.

Will paused near the back bumper of his pickup truck, hitched his thumbs in the belt loops of his khaki trousers and began to rock on his heels. "Afraid I haven't stayed put through the night since your mother passed on."

Jake's broad shoulders stiffened beneath his frayed blue work shirt, caught between sympathy and irritation. "I'm sorry about that, Dad—"

"Aw, don't be," Will scoffed. "Probably just a sign of aging. I'm just trying to say I wasn't deliberately spying."

"Good. Then you won't deliberately draw this thing out, either. I already filled in the blanks for you. You know the hows and whys—"

"It's bound to be only the beginning—for all of us!"

Jake shifted his weight from one leg to the other. "Aw, Dad…"

"Why'd you buy those gifts in the first place?" Will demanded, stepping up to give him a nudge between the shoulder blades. "You were so critical of the Parnells for trying to bribe Nadine with those roses on Sunday."

"It wasn't meant as a bribe," Jake denied, staring down into the creamy enamel. "Charmaine was my first concern at the time. She'd made it clear that she wanted the teddy, pointed it out in Ruby's window. The hankies were an afterthought so Nadine wouldn't feel slighted."

"Congratulations. Judging from her flighty step, I'd say Nadine pined for nothing."

Jake beamed in memory. "I'm sure she was more than satisfied."

The wrinkles in Will's face deepened. "You look disgustingly smug over what happened."

"Forgive me for feeling good this morning," Jake returned evenly. Hard as he tried, Jake couldn't dredge up much remorse in retrospect. Nadine had made him feel reckless and vital again. For the first time in ages, he felt as young as he truly was, felt in control of a moment in time. Nadine had put herself in his hands, and he'd pleased her and selfishly indulged himself in the bargain. It had been wonderful. If he could make Nadine see reason, understand that he wasn't happily-ever-after husband material, everything would be just fine. She needed a fine young buck without freight train tracks running down his soul. She was too fresh and new to settle for him—no matter how romantic he seemed right now.

"Guess there's nothing wrong in two adults agreeing to enjoy each other's company," Will went on to say, rubbing his chin. "Just so both parties have the same intentions…"

Jake carefully scraped excess paint off the flat stick, set it on the rim of the can and turned around. He stood toe-to-toe with his father, keeping his voice low. "You were the one who said the sisters are interchangeable."

"In the moonlight," Will clarified. "But the sun always rises, bringing everyday reality along with it. Now, you can't stand there and tell me you believed that those sisters would wake up with the same point of view on that kind of rendezvous."

Will was voicing the problem, all right, Jake mused with a sigh. He'd thought things through in the wee hours of the morning as he tossed and twisted in his narrow twin-size bed. If he'd only known in advance that she was virgin! The rest of the pieces concerning Nadine's motives would've clicked in time, before their lovemaking had gotten out of hand. After all, even he knew a woman's virginity was her most precious gift. And Nadine had chosen to give it to him, of all people. Why, for as long as he could remember, she'd been grounded in home and hearth, playing mother to her dollies, cooking imaginary meals on her toy stove. She had been saving herself for love, as she said. The one emotion he couldn't afford.

Will could tell he'd struck a nerve. "You should've put the brakes on—right off!"

Jake averted his eyes from his father's gaze. "I didn't pause to take a virginity poll. Let's just say I figured things out beyond the point of no return."

Will's eyes glinted grimly in full comprehension.

"It was like being caught up in a cyclone," Jake tried to explain, tearing a wrapper off a new paintbrush. "She was so thrilled that I wanted her, so impressed that I'd gotten her signals. I couldn't admit that I hadn't quite got the full impact."

Will heaved a sigh. "S'pose not."

"Eventually I didn't want to admit it anymore," Jake confided bluntly. With traces of a roguish smile, he threw the cellophane wrapper in the trash bin near the open garage door. "But please give me some credit, Dad. I wouldn't have given either one the teddy had I known Nadine was truly interested in me. I would never set out to deliberately disappoint her."

"Shape up and you won't disappoint her."

"Well, the least I can do is back away from Charmaine," Jake stated pensively. "We never got nearly as far, thank heavens."

"No matter what, Charmaine's bound to be a bit put out when she finds out what Nadine's done," Will cautioned.

"Thankfully, Nadine wants to keep things hushed up until after the hearing," Jake explained with a measure of relief. "At least that gives me some breathing space, time to find some answers." He shook his head, gazing out the door. "I should've given them both hankies."

"Smartest thing you've said all morning."

"Hush, now, Dad," he cautioned, catching sight of Amy Jo making her way toward the garage. Jake was the model of composure as he stepped out into the gravel driveway to meet his daughter. She was the picture of happiness and beauty as she skipped down the cracked walk leading from the rear of the house, dressed in a new oversized pink T-shirt and white knit shorts, carrying three textbooks in her small arms.

"All ready for school, honey?" he greeted, squatting to envelop her in a hug. He pulled her close and squeezed her hard, kissing each temple with a sound smack. He always overdid the goodbyes, something she had appreciated when it was just the two of them.

The bittersweet truth was that her attention was now focused in a hundred different directions. She gave him a peck on the cheek and tugged free. "I'm going to be late if I don't get going," she warned.

Jake smiled as he savored her transformation from clingy mouse to independent skylark. His delight over her progress far outweighed her rejection. "I just need a minute of your time," he teased.

Amy Jo released a short sigh. "For what, Daddy?"

"Well, for one thing, Grandpa and I are painting the house the color you asked."

She gasped in delight. "Will you be finished when I get home?"

Jake chuckled, giving her flowing black mane a tug. "Not quite."

She lifted her narrow shoulders. "Okay. Bye."

"Hey, hold on, speedy," he said, grasping her elbow. "This is the first I've seen of your new clothing."

She did a quick spin as he whistled appreciatively. "This outfit costed a lot of money, so you should like it," she announced matter-of-factly.

Jake reared back on his haunches. "You didn't have a lot."

"Grandma Thelma paid for everything," she breezily informed him.

"What!"

Amy Jo wasn't fazed much by Jake's thunderous response. The two girls waving from the end of the drive-way were her primary concern.

Will strolled up behind Jake. "Hurry on now, honey," he urged, blowing her a kiss.

"Paint the front of the house first!" she called out over her shoulder as she tore off down the gravel.

Jake felt Will's gnarled fingers sinking into his shoulder, as if urging him to take it easy. Jake rocketed to his feet just the same. "After all we shared last night, Nadine didn't say a word about Thelma," he bit out under his breath.

"You have the nerve to be self-righteous after your nightie switcheroo!" Will exclaimed in wonder.

Jake turned back the sleeves of his work shirt, flexing one fist, then the other. "I wasn't talking to you, Dad."

"No, you wouldn't want to hear the voice of reason right now."

"Smartest thing you said all morning." Jake charged across the lawn and plowed through the gap between the hedge and the fence, doubling its size in seconds.

Nadine was standing in the front foyer applying lipstick when she heard the back screen bounce on its hinges. She assumed that Charmaine had forgotten something and had backtracked home. Nadine had been so glad to finally be rid of her. Big sister had been a royal pain all through breakfast, slamming things as she muttered on and on about the stupid handkerchiefs the bonehead male next door had given her.

Understandably, Nadine jumped a mile when she caught sight of Jake's huge form, bursting out of tattered denim, barreling up the hallway. "Mornin', darlin'," she lilted in relief as she applied a second coat of coral-colored lipstick, identical to the shade of her A-line dress. "I didn't expect to see—"

She cried out as he grabbed her arm and brought her flush against him. The move caught her so off balance that her lipstick line veered off her mouth and down her chin. One glimpse of his murderous expression and she dropped the plastic cylinder altogether, sending it clattering to the hardwood floor. She knew she had to look a sight, but apparently not silly enough to temper Jake's thunder one bit.

There was only one explanation for the depth of his anger. Amy Jo had spilled the beans about Thelma Parnell's generosity. She'd seen the girl passing by the house a moment ago in one of the outfits Thelma had chosen.

"Can we talk about this calmly?" she requested anxiously.

"How could you let that woman move in on my child!" he roared, giving her a shake.

It took all of Nadine's self-control to look into his chrome-plated eyes and accept that last night's passion was replaced by hundred-proof fury.

"I know what you must think," she said placatingly, lightly touching his chest.

"Do you really?" he challenged in a dangerous whisper. "I'd say you don't look near frightened enough!"

"Oh, Jake!" Nadine's apprehension softened to sympathy as traces of raw fear danced around the edges of his eyes. "It's not like I encouraged Thelma's company, drew her into Buttons 'n' Bows for girl talk."

"The moment you saw her you should've turned on your heel and marched off."

"But I didn't see her!" she protested with a toss of her head. "It was simply a series of circumstances that went wrong. First, your credit didn't cover all the things, then I was short of cash. Ruby demanded payment in full, so I ran home for our household cache. I finally returned to find that Grandma Thelma had taken over the whole purchase.''

''Dammit!'' Jake abruptly released her and stalked around the cramped foyer. Nadine always seemed to throw a different light on everything that went on. He'd see it one way, and she'd rearrange it to her favor.

''It would've upset Amy Jo if I'd put up a fight,'' she pointed out.

''You shouldn't have left her alone in that crazy shop!'' was all he could think to say.

''That's nonsense,'' she said in mild disgust. ''Ruby's like extended family. Dysfunctional family, maybe,'' she added beneath his glare, ''but quite capable of watching over her for a short time. Face it, Jake, you can't wrap Amy Jo in a cocoon and expect her to thrive.''

''Now Thelma can bring that sales slip to the hearing and tell Judge Trimble that I couldn't afford to clothe my own daughter!''

''I know it.'' With a reluctant sigh, Nadine reached down for the open-ended lipstick that had stalled near the parson's bench. Her purse was on the bench, as was the cap to the lipstick. Needing time to think, she busily recapped the tube, dropped it in her handbag and pulled out a tissue. ''I'm not about to argue that Thelma is overstepping,'' she said in a melancholy voice, keeping her back to him, ''but surely you can see that I'm innocent.''

''My guess is that she's been just waiting for a chance to connect with Amy Jo,'' he returned tersely. ''Keeping your guard up wouldn't have hurt.''

''If Thelma's been hanging around town waiting for an opportunity, I think she would've pulled something sooner or later,'' Nadine asserted poutily.

Jake pounded his own hand. "A few more days and we'd have had this licked! Why, the hearing is scheduled for this Saturday morning at ten."

Nadine turned slowly toward the mirror tacked inside the closet door without meeting his eyes, unable to handle the betrayal still certain to be stamped there. "Jake," she began on a strained note, "you're blowing this way out of proportion. Judge Trimble is a wise man. He'll be looking for a loving environment for your child, not a lavish one." There was a lapse of silence to follow. Aware that she was already late for class, Nadine began to dab at the streak of lipstick running along her chin.

"You really think so?"

Nadine smiled into the mirror as Jake joined her in the reflection. "Yes. Everyone knows how the Parnells raised Rosemary. She wasn't happy surrounded with material things and having all her decisions made for her."

"No, I made her happy," Jake proclaimed proudly. "I let her be happy."

"That's wonderful, Jake. But I'm not convinced the Parnells ever meant Rosemary any harm," she couldn't resist adding in an effort to be fair. "Seems to me you two took off without clearing the air."

Jake knew that. But their bitterness had been so deep that it had taken years to wonder if they'd been unjust. He wasn't about to risk his daughter's well-being to find out. The Parnells were asking way too much. It was always the extreme with them. Total custody; total control. But it was no use rehashing these facts with Nadine. She knew them full well. "You always give them so much credit!" he roared in disappointment. "Can't you just stand with me?"

She offered him a sympathetic smile. Not in good conscience, she couldn't. Jake had blown his in-laws' faults way out of proportion over the years. Rosemary's death, of course, had given the feud the saddest of endings for both sides. But Jake was in no condition to listen to reason. Helping him to hang on to his faith was all she could hope for right now. "I wish you'd trust me," she finally pleaded. "Completely. Totally. As you did last night."

Soothing waves of comfort flooded over Jake, dousing the last of his flaming temper. She would fight dirty, he inwardly griped. How sneaky to bring up their consummation, remind him of how satisfied and fulfilled he'd felt under her spell. Though he was still dead set against another commitment, he understood that he'd taken giant steps in that direction. He and Nadine were bound together. Not in the traditional rice-and-wedding-cake way, of course, but they were a team beyond question.

With an awkward gesture, Jake turned her around, took the tissue from her hand and gently began to wipe away her coral smudge. "Guess I'm out of practice at looking to a woman for help."

Her mouth curved invitingly. "It's part of the deal, darling, being there for each other."

Jake's fingers trembled on her chin. He was as nervous as a young buck at his first dance. "I'll do better, honey. With everything."

"I know it," she purred, kissing the fingers at her mouth. "Just remember that I'm crazy in love with you."

"Or maybe just plain crazy." Jake shuddered as she burrowed close. His heart didn't understand his mind's stubborn stand on a commitment-free future; nor did his hands and mouth as they came to rest in her soft tide of hair, hungrily enjoying her sweetness. It was as though Nadine knew just what kind of woman best suited him—

sturdy, yet fragile; steely, yet vulnerable; proper, yet sexy. How clever of her to set a trap for him by being that woman! If only he weren't such a cynical, troubled kind of man...

"Oops! It seems I've dropped my handkerchief!"

Jake was balanced on an aluminum ladder later in the day, painting the eaves of the Flynn saltbox, when Charmaine's staged squeal of dismay pierced the tranquil air, sending birds skimming and squirrels scampering. He gazed down into the front yard, where she stood studying the pink square of fabric at her feet, then raised his eyes to the cloudy sky with a grimace. She wasn't going to rest until she turned his chaste, misdirected gift into something intriguing.

"Afternoon, Charmaine," he called out in a pleasant voice. "Home from work already?"

"I am, and I can tell you I'm having a terrible time keeping hold of my hankie," she lamented, giving her fingers a helpless flutter.

Jake clenched his teeth and the paintbrush in his hand. What a time to play a helpless Southern belle. He knew it was a flirty move, an invitation to play. Just as she knew he was far too busy for games right now! But Charmaine wasn't known for her patience or her sensitivity. She saw something, she grabbed for it.

Jake gave his head a rueful shake. How simple that kind of carefree mating had seemed only a few short days ago. But now he had new responsibilities. A woman he cared for loved him, trusted him—and fully expected him to stay away from this big sister. As he'd told Will, it was exactly what he intended to do.

"Jake Flynn, are you glued up there, or have you lost all traces of gallantry!"

One trait the Jordan sisters shared for sure was their persistence. "Coming!" Jake secured his brush on the rim of the paint can and descended the stainless-steel ladder. He crossed the space of lawn between them, tearing off his work gloves.

"You look mighty busy," she commented, her lips curving sweetly.

"So nice of you to notice." With a waist-deep bow, he hooked the handkerchief on his finger and presented it to her.

"You don't think I called you down here just to fetch, do you?" she pouted, fluttering her gold lashes.

Jake couldn't help but watch her stuff the lacy bit of fabric into the plunging neckline of her white, body-hugging minidress. She always did know how to display her assets to advantage. But there was a line drawn between explicit behavior and coyness that Charmaine never could discern. A line that Rosemary had never come close to. A line that Nadine somehow gracefully toed without ever stepping over!

Jake set his hands on his trim hips, straining for patience. "What's on your mind, Charmaine?"

"As if you can't guess," she teased, giving his pecs a nudge that would've sent a lesser man reeling.

Jake's body and expression showed his impatience. "I don't have time for guessing games."

Charmaine's full chest puffed on a sigh. "I figure it's high time you took a break. Will says you've been out here all day."

Jake stole a look at the Jordans' house beyond the black wrought-iron fencing, wondering if Nadine was watching them. "I'm anxious to finish the front of the house tonight," he hedged. "Promised Amy Jo."

"Oh, you can spare a few minutes for a glass of lem-

onade,'' she scoffed. Turning a deaf ear to his stream of
excuses, she began to unbutton his chambray shirt.

"What are you doing?" he squawked, brushing her
fingers away from his white plastic buttons.

"You can't hope to rub shoulders with me if you're
covered with paint," she complained.

"All right," he grumpily conceded, but removed the
shirt himself and set it on a lilac bush. "But the spattered
pants stay right where they are."

"For now, anyway." With a wink she linked her arm
in his and tugged him down the walk, keeping her hips
set in neutral to avoid contact with his yellow-blotched
pants.

Jake raised a sardonic brow as they climbed the Jordans' porch steps. Charmaine had been sure of herself.
Two tall frosted glasses of lemonade were ready and
waiting on a small pine table, and newspaper was spread
out on the bench swing.

"I feel like a yet-to-be-housebroken pooch," he
joked, settling back on the papers. His broad bare back
glistened with sweat and stuck to the back of the swing.

"It's nothing that a strip and a shower wouldn't
cure," Charmaine purred as she sank down beside him,
taking care with her pristine dress.

Jake swallowed hard and raised a hand to his forehead. "It's sure been a scorcher of a day."

"Let me cool you down," she crooned. With a flourish she produced a pale blue hankie from the cleft between her breasts.

Jake's eyes grew as he stared at the cotton square.
"Thought you had the pink one."

"I have all of them on me," she confided close to his
ear. "Thought you might want to play some hide-and-
seek." She dragged the lacy square down his chest and

stuffed it in his waistband below the navel. "Now, this first one's on me. That leaves five to seek out."

His eyes widened. "I can't do that!"

"You would've ten years ago," she protested with a pout. "Remember all the fun we used to have in that old car of Will's?"

"We were just kids!"

"We ain't exactly over the hill, sugar."

Jake lurched forward as her pale hand came to rest on his glistening copper shoulder, covering up his rebuff by grabbing a glass from the table. Charmaine was forced back to her side of the swing as he arched his arm to take a long sip of lemonade. Even that proved to have its price, he quickly came to realize with a jolt. Lemonade was not one of Charmaine's specialties. He coughed and sputtered over its tartness, his throat closing in self-defense.

Sometime during his coughing fit, Nadine waltzed out the door, still dressed in the coral dress she'd worn to school. "Brought you a spoon," she announced brightly. Edging her body between the table and swing, she covertly dropped two sugar cubes in the tall glass and gave it a brisk stir.

"Always looking out for me," he observed with a grateful smile.

"Never too far off," she replied pertly, plopping down between them on the slatted bench. Giving the floor a push with her feet, she got the swing moving on its creaky chains.

Charmaine folded her arms across her chest in disgust. "If we wanted to rock, we'd be doing it."

Nadine's voice pealed with laughter. "Oh, lighten up." Spying a tip of the blue hankie in Jake's waistband, Nadine tugged it out and pressed it to her moist hairline, smiling at her aghast sister. "Pardon me, both of you, but I am so overheated. I've been making sweet-potato bread—"

"You have?" Jake enthused, his hand unconsciously squeezing her knee. "I haven't had that since...I don't know when."

Nadine grinned. She remembered every recipe he'd ever loved. Preparing them would be her pleasure, for years and years to come. "I'll send some along for your supper if you like," she offered, much to Charmaine's slack-jawed affront.

His gray eyes glowed. "Thanks!"

"Let's just go check on that bread, shall we?" Charmaine suggested, popping up from the swing. "Excuse us, Jake."

Once alone, Jake released a shaky breath. It wasn't going to be easy to sort this out. Obviously Charmaine wasn't about to accept a simple rebuff, not when she had the nerve to stuff a hankie down his pants in broad daylight! She was in heat and hoping to relive the thrill and excitement of their youth. A few short days ago, it had been exactly what he'd wanted, too, but today that kind of reckless play seemed unworthy, now that Nadine had drawn him in with her sweet, honest affection.

Jake forced himself to face the facts. It was only a matter of time before Charmaine discovered she was the odd one out in the triangle. Despite their pact to keep their lovemaking a secret, Nadine wore the radiant glow of newfound passion like a badge of honor.

The only thing he could count on right now was that he was in trouble. Deep, deep trouble.

"Nadine, I really didn't want to help you with the bread," Charmaine confessed as they entered the hot, aromatic kitchen at the back of the house.

Nadine could barely contain her amusement. "You didn't?"

"No, I just want you to know that I've noticed your new attachment to Jake."

Nadine swallowed hard and fussed with her oven mitts on the counter. She wasn't ready for Charmaine to know the whole truth. Aside from her role in the custody situation, Nadine was still feeling vulnerable, unsure of the depth of Jake's feelings for her. Being confronted by his anger first thing this morning hadn't been especially good for her morale! It seemed wise to deepen the bond between them before testing it on her sultry sister.

"I wouldn't be pressing you so hard," Charmaine went on to say in hushed urgency, "if it weren't for the teddy."

Nadine whirled with a hammering heart. "Charmaine—"

"Let me explain," her sister directed with a raised palm. "I noticed it gone from Ruby's window, you see."

Nadine's forehead puckered in apprehension. "You speak to Ruby?"

"Why, of course! Nothing blunt, just said the window seemed empty without it."

Nadine's green eyes darted around nervously. "What did she say?"

"Well, she laughed," Charmaine reported with a measure of bewilderment. "You know that sly chuckle she has. Why, you'd have thought she believed it to be right there under my dress."

That did seem odd. But Nadine couldn't help but wonder how much the wishful Charmaine had read into the cryptic exchange. She struggled for an airy tone. "Ruby say anything flat out, or did she just keep dancing in circles?''

Charmaine studied her manicured nails with a sigh. ''Said it wasn't her place to discuss transactions of an intimate nature. Then looked at me as though I was supposed to be impressed with her discretion. Naturally, I didn't push her. If she didn't want to reveal the buyer, there wasn't much more I could do, without looking like a nosy spinster.''

''You were wise to leave it be—''

''Hell, no,'' Charmaine hooted. ''I'm just getting to the best part! I marched straight out to the alley and spoke to Buddy instead. Actually smoked one of his smelly old cigarettes just to soften him up. Finally, I flat out asked him if Jake bought that teddy.''

Nadine's features tightened. ''And?''

She clasped her hands together with an exquisite sound. ''He confirmed it, Nadine. Said Jake definitely wanted his new girl to have it.''

Nadine inhaled sharply. That damn Buddy! His idea of fun had always been one form of trouble or another. ''Now Char—''

''Now yourself!'' Charmaine snapped back. ''I don't want you interfering with my romance.''

''But Jake might not—''

Charmaine planted her hands on her hips. ''Look here, I'm a lonely woman these days. Hungry for things you can't even imagine.''

''Can't imagine?'' Nadine repeated bitingly.

''I'm sure your time for romance will come,'' Charmaine said in a patronizing tone. ''Maybe one of the Luther brothers—''

''They wear their caps backward,'' Nadine sputtered.

"They have burping contests at the drugstore soda fountain!"

Charmaine wrinkled her nose. "Maynard Junior isn't so bad."

Nadine's mouthed dropped open as she gasped for air. "Is that what you think of me?"

"You're a simple person with simple aspirations," Charmaine returned matter-of-factly. "Now, don't get all huffy. I'm not insinuating that you're trying to steal Jake away. I just think you've carelessly stumbled upon us too many times now, and I'm losing my patience."

Nadine could hardly control her anger. She jammed on her oven mitts and turned to the stove to busy herself. "Charmaine," she began as she eased the loaves out of the oven, "I suggest you slow down. Let Jake meet you halfway if that's what he intends to do."

"I'm telling you flat out to give us space," her sister snapped back. "We can't ignite our romance with all this interference from the families."

Nadine gave her a mocking look. "Kindly excuse us!"

Charmaine made a disgusted sound. "Well, things are going to be different, starting with the traveling carnival this weekend. One way or another, Jake's going to be my date. He must be aching to give me that lingerie by now, and I'm going to give him ample opportunity to do it!"

Nadine almost told Charmaine that Jake intended to take Amy Jo to the carnival as a reward for enduring the tutoring sessions, then Charmaine's reference to Maynard replayed itself in her head. Charmaine deserved to stumble around on her own.

## 9

"You carrying lead weights in here?"

Nadine smiled brightly at Will as he hoisted her heavy blue cooler into the trunk of the sisters' silver four-door sedan the following Friday evening. "I swear you say that every year!"

"Part of our little carnival-night tradition, I guess," the wiry old man returned with a wink. "You buy the sodas for the schoolchildren and I complain about lugging them around."

She gave his shoulders a squeeze. "Isn't it fun?"

His tanned face flushed with pleasure. In her aqua culotte dress, her strawberry hair loose around her shoulders, Nadine was a vision of femininity. "Wouldn't change a thing, not a thing," he claimed. *Unless to set a wedding veil on your head and escort you up the aisle to wed my son.*

"This year is even better, with more family to enjoy it all. And what a perfect incentive for Amy Jo," Nadine added, her voice dropping to a whisper. "She worked hard all week and her test scores today reflected it. They're already in Judge Trimble's hands so he can review them before the hearing tomorrow."

"I imagine Thelma Parnell submitted her sales slip

from Buttons 'n' Bows," Jake inserted, joining them at the back of the car.

"I have plenty of ammunition planned for my court appearance," Nadine assured with a pat to his arm.

Will's eyes darted nervously to his granddaughter, running a stick along the Jordans' spiked fence. "If nothing else, we'll just have to bring Amy Jo in to give her slant."

"I hope you don't have to do that," Nadine protested. "We've kept it from her all this while. It would be a shame to upset her now."

Jake's lips thinned in a sober line. Nadine did have his little girl's well-being at heart when she strived to keep this distressing fight from her. But Jake knew Nadine was also thinking of the Parnells, hoping to preserve their image in Amy Jo's eyes, so the child wouldn't begin to hate them. Jake had been secretly apprehensive about it all week long. He kept envisioning Nadine at the hearing, trying to be impartial, forgetting just how damaging a misplaced remark might be. Perhaps it was silly, but he felt incredibly vulnerable pitted against the town's leading citizens. Being in the right might just not be enough. Nadine was supposed to be his secret weapon!

The trio looked up as Charmaine sashayed out the Jordans' front door, dressed in scandalously short cutoffs and a blue gingham blouse.

"So who's going to give Charmaine the bad news about her plans for two being expanded to include all of us?" Will wondered, backing up a step to distance himself.

"I suppose I should explain that this isn't a date for her and me," Jake said with open reluctance.

"It's my responsibility," Nadine said with a sigh, setting her shoulders back. "I should've done it Tuesday when she laid down the law in the kitchen."

"But that crack about Maynard Junior must've hurt you bad," Will consoled her. "You weren't in the mood to play peacemaker."

"So now she thinks she's going to snag me up on the Ferris wheel, I bet. Just like— Never mind," Jake broke off abruptly as a flash of vivid green envy leapt into Nadine's large eyes. He'd been avoiding both the sisters, and it made for an unhappy triangle.

As Charmaine moved closer to the street, Will conveniently remembered that he'd left his wallet in the house and trotted back toward the freshly painted canary-yellow saltbox.

"Charmaine's blown my initial friendliness way out of proportion," Jake ventured to say, shifting from one boot to the other with an awkward shuffle. "I've been keeping my distance, and she's perceived it as a game, thinks I'm playing hard to get."

Nadine reddened in discomfort. Hard to get just about covered Jake's new attitude, all right. She hadn't managed to corner him again, either. Nadine had seen him each and every night, of course, before and after her sessions with Amy Jo. But to her surprise and frustration, he'd never suggested another sexy rendezvous. Oh, how she yearned to make love to him again, revel in the sensations so wonderful and new. As frustrated as she was, however, she hated to see him punish himself for Charmaine's heightened interest.

"You know, Jake, I think I can explain Charmaine's relentless pursuit," she slowly admitted.

Jake's brows jumped in surprise. "What do you mean?"

"Last Tuesday, when we went in to check on the bread—"

"You already explained that Charmaine warned you off me," he cut in. "About how she paired you with Maynard."

"Well, there's more to the story," Nadine confessed, nervously toying with the elastic watchband on her wrist.

Jake cast a harried glance at Charmaine, who'd paused at the fence to speak to Amy Jo. "Like what, honey?"

"Like she noticed the teddy gone from Ruby's window."

"Ruby wouldn't tell her anything!" Jake hissed. "Would she?"

"It wasn't Ruby." Nadine squeezed her eyes shut as she blurted out the worst. "Buddy confirmed that you bought it."

Jake slapped the base of his palm to his forehead. Damn that Buddy Davis. He would be one of only three people on earth who knew the teddy was meant for Charmaine. Had the do-less spilled that big bombshell? he wondered with a hammering heart. Once Charmaine started fishing, Buddy had to realize that Nadine had gotten the wrong box. But Buddy must've kept that secret, he deduced. The sisters would be wild with anger by now if they knew the whole truth.

Jake was filled with a wary irritation as he realized that Buddy Davis was a key player in his little deception. What would the envious loafer do with the information he had?

"Charmaine thinks you're just waiting for the chance to hand over the teddy," Nadine went on to report. "That's why she's being so pushy." She clasped her hands under her chin. "Oh, Jake, I'm so sorry I kept that secret from you. I promise it will be the one and only time it happens.''

Jake offered her a wan smile. She was apologizing to him! The better she treated him, the bigger heel he became.

As it turned out, their reluctance to explain the group's carnival plans to Charmaine found its own resolution. Amy Jo innocently did the honors near the Jordans' front gate. Nadine surreptitiously studied them, with a good notion of what was being said. As the child grew more animated, Charmaine stiffened visibly, until her curvy body was wooden beneath her shorts and blouse. It was clear that big sister had discovered they'd all be sharing Jake tonight.

''Does this make us a couple of chickens,'' Jake asked in a rueful baritone, sidling up to close the trunk with a thump. ''Letting a little girl give such bad news to such a big bad one?''

''I see us as practical adults,'' Nadine answered with new humor in her tone. ''Amy Jo is the only person here that Charmaine wouldn't stomp all over.''

Jake laughed. ''Guess you're right.''

''Teacher's always right,'' Nadine crooned. ''Whether it's you or me.''

Jake warmed with longing. Nadine had blossomed into a lovely caring woman, a prize few men deserved— least of all him. What she needed was a man without a face full of worry lines and a heart made of shoe leather.

He was tempted to give her shoulders a shake, tell her that playing around with him was a precious waste of her time. Town celebrations like the carnival were perfect opportunities to search out Mr. Right. But it was virtually impossible to follow through, when at that very moment she was making it clear to him that he was the one and only man for her.

Jake's jawline tightened as he struggled to fend off traitorous territorial feelings as her fingers skimmed over the soft surface of his white T-shirt. How easily she could arouse him! How desperately he wanted to make love to her again. But he simply couldn't afford to float into the vulnerable state that cocooned two people in a romantic cloud, making them think, live and breathe as one. Once the fog cleared the commitment was in place, and commitment was too risky. Losing Rosemary inch by inch, day by day, had been indescribably painful. After her death he'd vowed that he'd take minimal risks. It seemed the easiest way.

But it hurt like blazes to keep up his guard against Nadine's sexy, sweet overtures. It had to hurt her, as well, he realized. She seemed puzzled at the moment, unsure, a little resentful. Certainly with time her interest in him would ebb, the physical lightning would dim in her memory. She'd wonder why she'd fussed in the first place. He wondered how he'd be able to face her eventual disinterest. It seemed whatever path he took, he was going to endure further pain.

The carnival, as always, was being held on a farm owned by the city on the outskirts of town. A ride that should've taken a scant ten minutes stretched into a full half hour after a joyous Amy Jo confided to Nadine, seated at the wheel, that she'd promised to pick up a parcel of her girlfriends. Halfhearted scoldings came from the Flynn men, and a cry of indignation popped out of Charmaine. Nadine, accustomed to dealing with all the children concerned, barely batted an eye as they rolled through the quiet neighborhoods for a house-by-house pickup.

By the time Nadine eased to a stop in the roped-off parking area, the girls were singing at the top of their lungs, the men were humming along and her sulky sister had sunk into the center of the back seat with her hands over her ears.

"The dang ride over here was a carnival in itself," Charmaine muttered to Nadine as they all tumbled out of the vehicle. With whoops of joy the girls circled around, kicking up the dry packed dirt beneath their feet.

Nadine gave her key ring to Will so he could reach the cooler in the trunk. "I enjoy all this, Char," she confided. "Being around my students, absorbing their enthusiasm. I wish you would just go along with it for the sake of everyone."

Charmaine looked horrified. "We're glorified baby-sitters, is what!"

"Do you good, Charmaine," Will teased, pulling a couple of cans of soda out of the cooler. "Come and get it, girls!"

"Take along extras to pass along to your friends," Nadine instructed. She was about to help Will with the operation, when she felt Charmaine's hand on her elbow.

"I need to steal Nadine for a minute," Charmaine announced briskly.

With a shrug, Nadine allowed Charmaine to lead her through the rows of cars and over to a grassy area dotted with picnic tables. The carnival, set up five acres away, beyond the property's aging barn and house, livened up the landscape with colorful tents, a Ferris wheel and up-beat music. As inviting and nostalgic as it all was, Nadine could feel disturbing energies humming all around them. She was afraid there was no way to completely avoid trouble tonight.

"You know how important this night with Jake is to me," Charmaine hissed hotly, predictably launching into the one and only issue on her mind. "It's as though all of you are trying to sabotage the inevitable."

"That's not so!" Nadine emphatically denied. "I wish you'd give him a break, tonight of all nights, Charmaine. With the hearing, and all these children, romance may be the farthest thing from his mind."

"I'm good and tired of waiting," her sister huffily declared. "It can't hurt to tell him I know he purchased the teddy, that I'm more than willing to accept any and all proposals."

"You mustn't!" Nadine beseeched her, steepling her fingers in prayer.

Charmaine squinted suspiciously at Nadine's fervent expression. "Why not?"

"You'll only embarrass yourself, trust me."

Charmaine tossed her head back scornfully. "Never happened yet."

Nadine regarded her with a resigned sigh. "Oh, honey, I wish you weren't so set on Jake this way."

Charmaine gazed off down the winding county road, dotted with cars moving slowly toward the parking areas. "No reason not to be, when he's obviously set on me."

Nadine sank her teeth into her lower lip. "I have something to tell you. Something I should've told you last Tuesday—"

Charmaine seized her shoulders, her long manicured fingers digging into Nadine's flesh. "What on earth could you possibly know!"

Irritation over Charmaine's petulant stand gave Nadine's voice a sharp edge. "I had hoped this would keep through the weekend—"

"Keep?" Charmaine repeated in a lethal tone. "I'm good and mad this instant, Nadine Jordan, and sorely tempted to tip you upside down!"

"All right then!" Nadine retorted under her breath. "Jake bought the teddy, all right. For me."

Charmaine hooted in disbelief. "That's the kind of dream world you've been living in all week long? I knew you were acting funny, but it never occurred to me that you seriously considered yourself a contender for him!"

"I'm trying to caution you," Nadine persisted. "So you can put on the brakes."

Charmaine's eyes gleamed mockingly. "Little sister, you are a treasure. A simple-souled baby."

Nadine set her hands on her hips, determined to dislodge Charmaine's indifference once and for all. "Get this straight. He already gave me the teddy, way back when you got the handkerchiefs."

"That's ridiculous!" the older blonde sputtered.

Nadine laughed shortly. "Why?"

"Because you wouldn't even know what to do with it," Charmaine scoffed. "If you know what I mean," she added meanly, leaning closer.

"I knew exactly what to do," Nadine confided in a low triumphant purr. "Everything was a perfect fit, if you know what I mean!"

Charmaine's nostrils flared with fury as she glimpsed, for the very first time, traces of sophistication in her little sister's eyes. Her breath came in short gasps, her lush chest heaving beneath her gingham top. "You rotten little sneak!"

"I love him," Nadine confided. "Really love him."

"You never said a word! All week long, you never let on!"

"I figured I deserved a chance with him without your interference," Nadine flatly admitted. "And happily enough, it worked out fine."

Charmaine glared at her, emitting a panting sound.

Nadine was caught between sympathy and resentment. Charmaine was hurt, but she was so set on her own superiority. "You'll cool down and come to understand," she predicted, studying her nails.

Charmaine's eyes widened. "What makes you think I'm ready to give up?"

"It might be nice if just this once you didn't resort to being a sore loser," Nadine suggested.

Charmaine's head bobbed like a puppet's. "We'll just see, Nadine. We'll just see." With that she whirled around and stormed off in the direction of the carnival.

Jake had waved Will and the girls on to the festivities, then leaned a trim hip on the side of the car to watch the sisters, twin Venuses with their curvy bodies and tides of hair shining platinum in the setting sun. No doubt about it, Nadine was telling Charmaine about their encounter. And she wasn't one to mince her words. Within moments Charmaine was marching off, falling in behind the excited youngsters and spry Will.

He wasted no time moving forward to meet Nadine on the grassy slope.

"She was determined to confront you for a show-down, so I just had to tell her," she said. Her hushed voice was filled with distress. "As irritated as I've been with her, I couldn't let her make a fool of herself in public, mooning after you for all to see. It would've killed her later, when folks came to realize your romance wasn't meant to be.''

He angled an arm across her shoulders and gave her a squeeze. ''I know it. I should've done it myself.'' He stared off at Charmaine's retreating figure, frowning with uncertainty. ''Maybe I should catch up to her, try to explain.'' As if he could explain, Jake thought ruefully. His solo plans were bound to be very unpopular with everyone. If only he could make them understand that he'd already done battle in life's arena, survived by the skin of his teeth, and wanted little more than to raise his daughter in peace.

''No, don't bother with her,'' Nadine protested with genuine anxiety. ''Charmaine needs time to absorb the shock, decide how she wishes to handle things. You know—'' She broke off abruptly with a contrived cough. The fact that Charmaine was in denial, and still determined to win the battle, was a confidence that surely would keep a while.

''Guess we all could use some time to cool down,'' Jake jovially pointed out.

Nadine's mouth softened with a knowing smile. ''Not me, darlin'. I'm just heating up.''

Jake's body trembled from head to toe. That was what he was afraid of.

Keeping him in tow, she caught up with Will and the girls and suggested games of chance they might enjoy, such as knocking over bottles with balls, popping balloons with darts, flipping coins onto plates. They were back on the family track, with extra giggly girls in the bargain. Jake began to share his boyhood carnival memories with everyone. The girls were awestruck by his low, liquid voice, his handsome face, his towering figure.

He could clearly see that his daughter was accepted by her peers. Now, if only they could repel the Parnells.

The Parnells were present, of course, mingling with Cherry Creek's older generation, but they kept a close eye on Jake's group. He could see the hunger in Thelma's eyes as she and Calder passed by near the Tilt-A-Whirl and a hamburger stand. They grew more bold once Amy Jo waved to them as she worked her way down the row of open-fronted tents that held the games of skill and chance. He was deeply grateful that Nadine didn't try to include them out of sympathy. She simply nodded hello and turned her attention back to their group.

That left Jake with only one other worry—Charmaine. She was a loose cannon, wandering around the grounds, furious with him for rejecting her. He felt he probably deserved a tongue lashing, but he didn't want it here, in public, the night before the custody hearing.

It was a full two hours later when he finally met up with the older Jordan sister. It was as charmingly contrived as Charmaine herself was. He was standing alone at the concession stand buying a beer, when her red talons lighted on his solid tanned arm. He turned slowly, to find her face was as pink and soft as her cloud of cotton candy. Her hazel eyes shifted like an uncertain storm, first flickering darkly, then with seawater limpidness. "I want to speak to you, Jake Flynn."

"I...know you do." He lifted the tall paper cup to his mouth and took a long draw of the foamy brew.

She gave the dusty ground a hard stomp with her small leather shoe. "What on earth are you doing, toying with my little sister?"

"Will you please keep your voice down," he anxiously asked.

Her large red mouth was pulled tight with petulance. "You answer me, mister, or I'll scream the town down!"

There was a small beer garden situated behind the concession stand, and Jake scanned it for any curiosity seekers. The men seated at the small round tables were boisterous and lost in their own world, so he felt it was safe to lead Charmaine inside. She sat down at a small wobbly table set off by itself and he leaned against a fence post. Twilight was swiftly closing in, leaving the carnival in a muted light from the colorful light bulbs strung on every booth and tent.

"I never meant to upset you, Sassy," he rasped apologetically above the thumping music.

Charmaine opened her mouth and set a tuft of cotton candy on her tongue. She savored it for a long moment before swallowing. "I thought we had something real nice goin'. What happened?"

Jake slowly shook his head in the shadows, staring off into the velvet sky. "Nothing got started, Charmaine, not really."

The table jiggled as she pounded it with her fist. "But I wanted it to!"

He chuckled gently as the spoiled child inside her rose to the surface. "And we all know you're accustomed to getting exactly what you want."

"Damn straight!" she promptly agreed. "I love to win. It's one of my many endearing qualities."

"Hey! I've been looking all over…" Nadine came to halt just inside the garden, falling speechless at the sight of her sister seated behind the picket fence. From a distance it had appeared that Jake was alone. She'd hurried to him with hope in her heart and a skip in her step, thinking that just maybe he'd make love to her tonight after all.

Now her hopes were nose-diving as fast as they'd soared. She swallowed her disappointment and made an effort to keep her tone light. "Will is taking the girls home in my car. I told him we'd walk back or hitch a ride with someone else. If that's all right." She looked from Charmaine to Jake, wondering what they'd said to each other, just how much she'd missed. Their stiff silence and closed expressions made her uneasy. As in the past, they were sharing something that did not include her. Without even knowing if it was good, bad or somewhere in between, she longed to be part of it. Felt she deserved to be a part of it, now that she was his woman.

If she was his woman... Suddenly, every fiber of her being was stiff with uncertainty. Tension crackled in the air around them. Nadine felt threatened despite the cry of denial rising from her heart. Charmaine was primed for battle, and Nadine knew full well the extent of her artillery.

"You know, Charmaine," Nadine whispered firmly, "I hoped we could avoid a scene here. That's why I warned you off this chase in the first place."

"Chase," Charmaine hissed in withering disbelief. "I've never chased any man—ever! Why, I'd sooner give in to Buddy Davis than sink to begging any man."

Nadine let out a squeal of surprise as she felt fingers pinch her bottom. She spun around to find Buddy Davis standing behind her in ragged jeans and a black T-shirt boasting a fluorescent skull, holding a full paper cup of beer in his soft white hand. She chose not to reveal that he'd put a hand on her, for Jake's profile was already chiseled in stone.

"Did I hear you callin' me, Char?" he whined.

"Only in the confines of your vivid imagination," Charmaine retorted with a delicate sniff.

"That's not so nice," Buddy scolded on a belch.

"You look like a man who should be heading on home for a rest," Jake suggested levelly. It was a strain to keep his tone even when raw fear was knotting his chest. This do-less was the last person he cared to tangle with tonight, and Buddy knew it. His eyes held a dangerous glitter that was not entirely due to alcohol. He finally had some power over his greatest rival. He knew about the mishandling of the gifts.

"Ain't really tired," Buddy announced, sinking into the empty chair beside Charmaine. "But I outta be, with all the deliveries and such I do for Ma at the shop. You know the shop, don't ya, Jake? Buttons 'n' Bows, tigers 'n' toes, undies for the sister and hankies for the nose." He snorted with laughter, squinting up at his nemesis who was hovering overhead like a huge panther poised to pounce.

"I advise you to head on home, Buddy," Jake said curtly, flexing his huge hand.

"And miss the company of the two purtiest girls in town? Nosiree." He took a deep slurp of beer and wiped the foam off his mouth with the back of his hand. "I ever tell you lad—ladies that I enjoy making deliveries more than anything else in this whole world?"

"No, Buddy," Nadine replied shortly, folding her arms across her chest in an impatient gesture.

Buddy's face crumpled. "You don't want me round, neither, Nadine? After what I done for you?"

Charmaine shot him a sour look across the table. "What did you do for my sister?"

"Made her the happiest girl in town, that's what," he answered slyly. He reached out to give Nadine a pat on the hip, but she was quick enough to step out of his grasp. She bumped into Jake in the process and was surprised when he clamped a hand on her shoulder. The strength of his grip told her he was simmering with a raw anger that seemed way out of proportion to the awkward circumstances.

"See that?" Buddy challenged, gesturing at the sight of Nadine leaning into Jake's form. "I did that, Charmaine. Just to keep you free for me."

Nadine felt Jake's body stiffen like lumber beneath her soft body. The fact that Buddy was upsetting him brought her fully alert.

"I suggest you get a move on, Buddy," Jake directed tersely, no longer struggling to be civil.

"I'm goin'. But I just want 'em to know how clever I can be." Buddy awkwardly pointed to his own shallow chest. "How I make things happen."

Make things happen? Jake's brain flashed with startling revelation. There were no accidents here, after all. Buddy hadn't accidentally mixed up the gifts, just as he hadn't run into them tonight by chance. The do-less bastard had set him up! Jake's brain ticked madly. If only he could somehow make his escape with the sisters before the gift switch came to light. He could then corner Buddy at a later time, convince him to keep quiet forever.

"Let's get out of here, girls," Jake abruptly commanded. Without loosening his grip on Nadine's shoulder, he curled his fingers around Charmaine's upper arm, urging her up.

"Can't go yet," Buddy insisted, rising to his feet. "Not till we talk about the presents."

Jake released the women and stepped into Buddy's

space. "I am warning you, Buddy," he hissed for his ears alone. "Shut up until you sober up."

"Your time is up, buddy," the do-less cackled with glee.

"Buddy Davis," Charmaine huffed with her customary impatience. "You are the biggest fool that ever walked the countryside, and I am tired of your pining after me." She edged past the men to join Nadine at the garden entrance. "I don't want you now, or ever!"

"Oh yeah?" Buddy jumped and bobbed around Jake's sturdy frame to speak directly to the women. "Fool? We'll see who's the fool here. Delivered them presents nice and backwards is what I did. How do you like that?" He gestured to Jake with a flailing arm. "This—this fool here fell right into my trap. Finally got you good, Flynn, after all these years."

"What?" The blood drained from Nadine's face as the meaning of Buddy's ramblings became clear.

"Step aside, so I can tell the girls all about it," Buddy whined to Jake.

"Get lost," Jake ground out, blocking his path.

That was when Buddy made a huge mistake. He gave Jake a shove. It wasn't much of a shove, but it was excuse enough for the more powerful man to send the do-less flying with a right cross to his weak, stubbly chin. Buddy staggered back and fell into a table full of disgruntled old-timers who pushed him off with shouts of complaint.

"I knew it!" Charmaine rejoiced, dancing out of the beer garden. "You did mean to seduce me all along! Everything makes sense now. The prissy hankies were meant for our prim teacher. Oh, Jake, shame on you for letting me get away!" she scolded with a wagging finger and a naughty grin.

Jake had taken hold of Nadine's arm and could feel her slight body tremble beneath his touch. He tried to tighten his grip, but she slipped away, as though melting into nothing. Before he knew what was happening, she stumbled into the thoroughfare, intent on escaping anyone who might witness her anguish.

Nadine never looked back as she moved unsteadily along the lighted path leading to the parking lot and the road back home, wishing the earth would swallow her up. Could there be a deeper humiliation than to learn you'd forced yourself on a man who hadn't desired you in the first place?

Small things that had seemed unimportant at the time tumbled through her mind as she replayed their encounter in the gazebo. The way Jake had called her Sassy. The dumbstruck expression he wore when she pulled back her tide of hair to reveal her face to him. He'd covered up his shock with phrases like he "never expected it to be like this" and "can't believe you want me this much." All the while he had to be thinking, "How'd I end up in this mess?" These memories flashed before her, making her heart constrict in crippling pain.

"Stop, Nadine!" Jake called out. "Please."

Nadine reluctantly turned around as he overtook her on the path.

"I truly don't know who is the biggest fool in this charade, Jake," she croaked with a feeble attempt at laughter. "But this is one time we can count Buddy out of the running for sure."

"Oh, honey." His voice was a pleading caress. But she was determined he wouldn't touch her in any way, anymore. She kept her distance with a step back, her face a cold unreadable mask.

"I forgive you for making love to my sister," Charmaine generously chirped, skipping up to stroke the planes of his face. "We'll just call it a mistake, a misunderstanding."

"I won't have you calling it anything," Jake growled, brushing aside her hand. "Can't you see that such talk might be painful for Nadine?"

"She knows all's fair in the manhunt," Charmaine asserted, with a knowing lift of her chin. "Why, she was so sneaky that I didn't even believe she was in the game. No matter," she declared airily. "I've won the duel and therefore the husband!"

Jake reared back in shock. "I'm not some male trophy to be passed between the two of you."

"Trophy? Don't overestimate your worth," Nadine bit out, hot pressure burning the back of her eyes.

"I'm not!" he argued incredulously. "But I do have an objection to this manhunt. My intentions have never been marriage. I was simply looking for friendship from you both. I thought you understood—"

"Friendship!" the sisters exclaimed in unison, their eyes locking in disbelief.

"Yes!" he staunchly maintained. "We've always gotten on well."

"Well, slap the dog 'n' spit in the fire!" Charmaine squealed. "Jake wants a couple of pals. What do you make of that, Nadine?"

"I don't...know," she faltered, her eyes downcast. Was this as much her fault as his? She'd have to think it over with her characteristic caution. The one and only time she'd drawn a hasty conclusion had left her in this embarrassing position!

Charmaine felt no need to dig deep for her feelings on the matter. "To think I was all set to marry you, Jake

Flynn!'' she huffily proclaimed, tightening the knotted gingham shirttail at her navel. "Planned out the whole thing on paper. Put the preacher in readiness."

"How dare you?" he challenged hoarsely. Galvanic anger surged through his system, flushing his face, cording his neck, bulging his eyes. "It's always been my understanding that it takes two people of sound mind to make those decisions!" He swiveled on his heel to Nadine, then back and forth, between the pair. "I'll never settle down again," he raged. "Not with anybody! And the two of you should know it! I—I never made any promises! Think about it!" With a bitter growl, he stomped back toward the carnival.

# 10

Nadine tossed and turned far into the night, finding it impossible to sleep. She knew it was foolhardy, but she couldn't resist moving to her bedroom window facing the Flynn property to take a peek across the way. An uneasy quiver tingled her spine as she noticed that Jake's light was on beyond the chiffon curtains. Was he hurting too? It would serve him right if he was losing some sleep along with her. She sat on the sill, hoping for a glimpse of life, a sign.

Nadine tipped her head back against the sill, and her lashes dropped slowly to her tear-stained cheeks. There were so many things she wanted to say to him now. Once the shock of Buddy's revelation had worn off, her good sense had taken over. She would never rest until the air between them was cleared.

"Hey."

His husky greeting startled her. Her eyes snapped open and she found herself face-to-face with the wildest looking version of Jake she'd ever seen. He was framed in the glowing screen across the way, his black hair tousled, his bare chest heaving. Why did she find him so sexy when she was so furious with him?

"You speaking to me, Nadine?" he gently prodded.

She lifted a thin shoulder beneath her gauzy nightie. "Hey yourself, I guess."

He braced his arm on his window frame with a deep sigh. "I'm sorry, honey. I never meant for things to turn out this way."

Her forehead puckered in a frown. "What part are you sorry for, Jake? For making love? For getting caught in your lies? Just what are we fightin' here?"

"You sure make a man think," he complained with a trace of humor.

She fluttered her hand over her chest. "Be still, my heart. I drive a man to think."

"I admit I handled things poorly. I thought that Charmaine was open to a little fun and decided to buy her the lingerie."

"And thought I was open to a runny nose and bought me handkerchiefs!" she cried out.

"Quit putting words in my mouth," he objected. "Just because I never viewed you as a lover doesn't mean that you weren't a dynamite one."

She sighed softly, twirling some of her berry-blond hair around her finger. "I hoped it was the beginning of something special."

"I know that you did," he confessed. "But I have serious reservations about marrying again. I just wasn't operating with that intention."

"You knew I was, though," she accused. "Maybe not as we made love, but certainly after I told you I loved you. Remember me saying those words?"

"Yes, honey, but—"

"And you had all week to speak to me, to set me straight. But oh, no, you even let me tell Charmaine that I'd gotten the teddy instead of her!"

"I didn't know you were going to do that tonight! We

agreed it would be a secret. I thought we'd settle it together and no one else would need to know.''

''You let it go too far, Jake,'' she asserted flatly. ''Inexcusably far.''

''But it was all so touchy. You feel things deeply, I realize that. And it was your first time—a shock to me, Nadine. Can't you accept that I was helpless and confused? Overwhelmed with my battle for Amy Jo?''

She nodded, her expression grim. ''So your main goal was to string me along until tomorrow when I report to Judge Trimble. I hoped that wasn't true.''

He made an incredulous noise. ''There you go again, speaking for me.''

''Well, it seems you can't get much done on your own, doesn't it? Can't even get underwear delivered to the right place!''

He could only imagine how humiliated she felt by the mix-up. It was more than enough to put her off him, which, ironically, was what he'd wanted. But he didn't want things to go bad this way. ''I—I fervently wish the circumstances had been different,'' he said desperately. ''But I've been on the marriage-go-round once for the spin of my life, and plan to settle for my memories. I should've made that clearer. I'm sorry I didn't.''

''Your circumstances aren't your problem, Jake, it's your handling of them.''

His silhouette stiffened in the light. ''I don't see how.''

No, he couldn't, she realized with equal measures of loathing and pity. He was so frightened of living now that he already had one foot in the grave. But he wasn't able to reason his way out of his fears, and she wasn't in the mood to help the lying bugger.

"If you have something to say, Nadine," he prodded, "I wish you'd just say it."

"All right! You're too cautious with your heart, too stingy with your affection—and too dense between the ears to realize it!" With a disgusted huff, she leapt off the sill and slammed the window down.

Jake strode into the county courthouse the next morning feeling calm and determined. When he entered the room where the hearing was to be held, he flinched; everyone seated in the small informal room was dressed to the teeth. The Parnells were in crisp linen suits, as was a dapper man who had to be their Savannah attorney, Milton Soames. Nadine was in an emerald dress that matched her eyes. Even Ruby Davis, in a gaudy rayon two-piece dress with pleated skirt, had outdone herself. He hadn't expected Ruby, but he should have, considering that she had to somehow avenge her precious Buddy. She was baring her teeth along with the rest of them.

Jake, more informally dressed in black cotton slacks and a gray pin-stripe shirt, surveyed the group of people assembled because he was forced to fight for his daughter, and kept his temper buried by concentrating on how chipper his daughter had been at breakfast when she announced that Will was taking her to the movies. Funny, how calm he felt right now. After the emotion-packed week he'd spent, he suddenly felt an uncanny peace inside himself. He was a good man who deserved his daughter—that was the bottom line.

"All rise!" Judge Trimble made the announcement himself as he slipped through a back door and up to the podium that had served as his bench for the past thirty years.

Jake moved quickly to the front table on the left, across from the Parnell camp. Nadine and Ruby were seated together in the background. It made Jake uneasy. Was the lovely schoolteacher so angry that she'd sink his ship?

The judge invited Thelma and Calder Parnell to state their case. They did so through Milton Soames, who rambled on about Jake's financial difficulties, his long working hours in Ohio, his plot to keep Rosemary and the child, Amy Jo, from the Parnells.

Nadine watched Jake with open distress. Did he understand they were trying to provoke him? Did he know that Ruby was here to attest to his temper?

He certainly did. Despite the mental work he'd done to present himself as a cool and reasonable person, he couldn't help but smolder over the attack on him. It didn't take long for him to shoot out of his chair, hot on the defense. "I don't live in Cleveland anymore," he argued. "And Rosemary was an independent woman. I never bossed her around."

The judge shook his gavel at Jake. "Wait your turn."

Jake waved his hands helplessly. "But I don't have an attorney to object."

Judge Trimble's gray eyes peered at him over his bifocals, his moon-shaped face stern. "I deeply appreciate it, too. This is one hearing that will not be dragged out with all sorts of poppycock. Let them state their case, then you will have a chance."

Jake slowly nodded and sank back in his seat. The attack forged on to paint him as an insensitive, selfish fiend. Ruby was introduced at the pinnacle of the argument and was asked to relate how Jake had punched her defenseless boy in the nose.

"It was in the chin, and he shoved me first!" Jake objected.

Judge Trimble hit his gavel. "Sit down!"

"He shouldn't have blamed my boy for the lingerie mistake," Ruby babbled on. She leveled a chunky finger at Jake across the aisle. "Maybe he shouldn't have been buying that sort of thing in the first place!"

Judge Trimble sent his gavel in a virtual tap dance to regain order. "I, for one, am grateful that somebody bought that red thing in your window," he announced sharply. "I was sick and tired of looking at it every time I walked down the street. And husbands in general were sick and tired of their wives asking them to dip into their savings to buy it!" He shook his bald head and turned to Jake. "All right, Jake. It's your turn to speak."

Jake stood and nodded to the judge. "I have little to say, really. I think it's ridiculous that the Parnells have taken this action to court at all."

"But we want to see our granddaughter!" Thelma jumped up to say.

"You want to own her," Jake corrected tersely.

Judge Trimble made a disgusted noise. "Simmer down, Thelma. Jake, address the court."

Jake cleared his throat, collecting his thoughts. Stick to the issues. Quell the temper and stick to the issues. That's what Nadine would say if she were speaking to him. He'd desperately hoped she would call this morning to offer support, but she hadn't. Knowing she was a wild card was the final straw on the camel's breaking back. "I came back here to raise my daughter among friends," he asserted as evenly as he could manage. "Yes, times have been tough for us since Rosemary fell ill. Amy Jo's struggled a bit in school and I had to sell my construction company. But there's no basis for a custody battle."

He shook his raven head. "Amy Jo has a loving family—my father and I. She's happy with us. There is nothing on the Parnell peanut farm that would enhance her life."

After he sat back down, the judge leaned forward at the podium. "Quite frankly, Nadine, I am anxious to hear your slant on things."

Nadine stood up, straightening her green dress. "You—"

"Please come forward," the judge requested, beckoning her forward.

Nervously, she moved to the front of the room. She had hoped to speak to Jake's back. It was bound to be easier than confronting his two-faced face.

"You have my report on Amy Jo's scholastic standing," she said, flexing her fingers at her sides, keeping her eyes straight ahead. She was standing right beside his table and could feel his eyes upon her. "It's my opinion that she is doing just fine."

The judge made a note. "Do you feel she is well adjusted in general?"

"As well as can be expected. Losing a mother is an awful blow for a child to bear."

"How does she measure up to her peers?"

"She is on a par with them," Nadine asserted proudly. "Amy Jo is definitely on the mend, Judge. She's tough and she's smart, and she's secure in her home environment."

Trimble nodded. "What is your overall opinion of the Flynn circumstances, Nadine?"

Jake rolled his eyes. Circumstances. The key word of last night's windowsill argument. Would she announce that she felt Jake wasn't handling his circumstances well at all?

Nadine inhaled, keeping eye contact with the judge. "I heartily recommend that Amy Jo remain with her father. I, too, believe this matter never should've reached court."

Cries of anguish and outrage erupted from the Parnell camp. Nadine turned to face them. "I don't mean anything against you," she assured them. "I understand why you are drawn to Amy Jo. After all, she's your granddaughter."

"But he's unfit!" Calder bellowed. "Let our Rosemary wither away."

Jake sprang up in affront. "I didn't! I loved her! When you love someone you don't go halfway. You bask in their love and return it. No matter what the cost, no matter what the circumstance—" Jake broke off, feeling Nadine's eyes upon him. He turned to meet her knowing gaze for a moment, then lowered his eyes in shame and discomfort. This was just the kind of thing she'd been trying to tell him. Just the stuff he'd been foolishly running from.

"Life is nothing without all the little strings of commitment that bond us together," he went on slowly, deliberately. He craned to confront the Parnells seated at the opposite table. "I did all I could for your daughter, believe me. She did want to come back, and had she lived, we would have!"

"We didn't know that!" Thelma gasped.

"Would you have believed me had I told you?" Jake challenged bluntly.

"I see that temper rising to the surface," Ruby intervened, her beady eyes bright. "Watch out or he'll slug you, Judge! You ask Nadine. She was there. See if my Buddy don't have a just complaint."

Judge Trimble rapped his gavel again. "Quiet!" He

turned his attention back to Nadine, still standing between the tables. "Is this temper thing an issue?"

Jake's heart slammed against his chest. This was her chance to repay him for the pain he'd caused her. Even if he won the battle for Amy Jo, he had the feeling that Buddy was going to sue him for something.

Nadine cleared her throat, mentally searching for the proper response. "Jake did punch Buddy," she admitted. "But he did it to protect my sister and me," she hastily added. "You see, Buddy was drunk and upsetting us. He even pinched my, uh, rear end. Jake repeatedly asked him to move on and he would not. In the end it was Buddy who got physical first. Jake only acted in self-defense."

The courtroom was hopelessly abuzz after that. Judge Trimble shouted that the case against Jake was dismissed and instructed Ruby to forget last night's altercation.

Nadine was literally running down the courtroom's concrete steps when Jake caught up with her. Her mouth formed an O of surprise and he couldn't resist kissing it soundly.

She accepted the kiss with aplomb. "Don't think I've weakened to your charms," she cautioned smoothly. "I merely told the truth. You're a good father, Jake. A jackass suitor, but that shouldn't cause Amy Jo any harm."

Jake gazed at her warmly, until her green eyes began to twinkle. "Pulling me out of the fire with Buddy was unnecessary charity, though," he persisted. "You had to have done that out of goodwill."

"Well…" She trailed off airily, staring into the sunny sky. "I told the truth there, too. Buddy was bothering us, and you did tell him to leave."

"Thank you," he said, deeply grateful. "I can't thank you enough."

"You're welcome." She tucked her lush mane behind her ears and moved down the last step to the sidewalk.

"I'm thanking you for more than you know," he went on, persistent at her side.

"Oh?"

"Didn't you get my message in there, Nadine?" he asked bleakly.

"Say what you mean," she urged, struggling to keep a quaver from her voice.

"I mean I've learned my lessons all over again," he told her with passion. "When you love someone, you can't afford to hold back." He raked a hand through his hair. "I know that's been your message all week long, teach. But I wasn't ready to see it until today, in court. Playing it safe with half a relationship would never be enough in the long run. When someone's absolutely perfect for a guy, he should play it smart and stake a claim. Tie her up for the rest of her life."

"I'm afraid Charmaine's had it with Cherry Creek," Nadine said teasingly. "She's planning an extended stay with our folks in Phoenix."

Jake frowned at her, squeezing her hands in his. "You're the perfect woman for me, Nadine. You even claim to love me with all my faults and shopworn viewpoint," he added ruefully. "Which makes you a real rare find—if it still holds true."

Nadine's mouth compressed as she thought things over. "You still haven't said it yet, you know."

He searched her eyes and asked plaintively, "What, woman?"

"That you love me," she answered in a small anxious voice.

"I love you Nadine!" he proclaimed for all to hear. "And not a day will go by that I won't talk about it.

Shout about it! Even after we've been married for years and years, I'll be telling folks how much I love you.'' He put his hands on her waist, lifted her in the air and spun her around.

''Stop it right now!''

His brows arched. ''Stop loving you?''

''Stop spinning me!''

He landed her gently and she collapsed onto his chest with gales of laughter. ''I happen to think you've loved me all week long,'' she teased, poking his chest.

''Yeah, but I wasn't listening to my heart at the start,'' he admitted. ''I'd have seen your true value right off if I'd faced my fears about starting over.''

They both gasped in surprise to find the Parnells had paused beside them on the sidewalk.

''Don't let this mislead you,'' Nadine ventured awkwardly, turning to the couple. ''I was as fair as I could be in court.''

Thelma nodded her perfectly styled head, her eyes growing misty. ''It isn't that at all, Nadine. We just wanted to tell Jake that we've come to believe that we've been too harsh with him. Seeing his anguish over Rosemary today, hearing him say that she wanted to return...'' She turned to Calder as she choked up.

''We were wrong to lay so much blame on you,'' Calder went on. ''And we've got eyes. We can see how Amy Jo is thriving here in Cherry Creek, surrounded by all the things we all love. We jumped the gun and we're sorry.''

''I guess I've held my grudge far too long, as well,'' Jake conceded, rubbing the back of his neck. ''It must've been hard to discover that Rosemary was pregnant so young. Nadine's been working on me all week to see your point of view, and I guess if she and I are going to be making a go of it, I'm going to have to listen to her advice.''

Everyone sighed, releasing the lingering tension. Thelma took Nadine's hand and squeezed it. ''This is fine news, dear, just fine. I can't think of anyone who would take better care of my granddaughter.''

''You won't be moving, will you?'' Calder asked abruptly.

''No, I imagine we'll settle in at my house after the wedding,'' Nadine replied. ''Right, Jake?''

''Sounds wonderful,'' he answered, kissing the top of her head. ''I know Amy Jo will be thrilled with the move.''

Nadine wrinkled her nose in confusion. ''Why?''

''Because she's already tiring of the canary yellow she chose for Will's house. Now she's talking tangerine.''

Nadine released an audible groan over the Parnells' amused chuckles. After exchanging goodbyes, she and Jake started strolling down the maple-shaded sidewalk toward home.

''Tangerine, you say?'' she queried, gazing up at his profile.

''Tangerine,'' he affirmed.

''Maybe we could let her loose in the gazebo,'' Nadine suggested. ''She could decorate that any way she liked without inconveniencing anyone.''

Jake turned to her with bedroom eyes and a huge wolfish smile. ''Let's set you loose in the gazebo first,'' he suggested silkily. ''Round midnight, maybe.''

She fluttered her lashes prettily. ''Why, Jake Flynn, it would be pitch-black out there at that time of night, too dark for decorating.''

''Ah, but the perfect time for another lesson in love,'' he said huskily.

The look she gave him transformed her into the nymph of the moonlit gazebo. "Promise to play teacher again, and this student will be right on time," she purred.

He reached for her joyfully and squeezed her close. "Bring along that polished ceramic apple from your desk, and I promise to take you straight to the head of the class."

* * * * *

## COMING NEXT MONTH

### THE SEDUCTION OF FIONA TALLCHIEF
### Cait London

*Man of the Month*

A Palladin man to marry a Tallchief woman? It was unthinkable—the families were long-burning enemies! But Joel Palladin had watched Fiona Tallchief's fiery beauty from afar and was determined to have her—whatever the cost...

### THE PRINCESS BRIDE Diana Palmer

Tiffany Blair vowed to walk down the aisle as Kingman Marshall's bride. King thought marriage was for fools! But he'd give anything to carry sheltered Tiffany over the threshold to womanhood...

### THE BABY NOTION Dixie Browning

*Daddy Knows Last*

Jake Spencer liked the way babies are made—but wasn't planning on making one himself. Until he overheard that the sexiest girl in town was planning a trip to the sperm clinic... Could he convince Priss to do her baby-making the old-fashioned way?

### BEAUTY AND THE BRAIN Elizabeth Bevarly

*Comet Fever*

Be careful what you wish for! Too bad, Rosemary March hadn't heeded this advice fifteen years ago. She'd asked for brainy Willis Random to meet his match, now he had—and it was her!

### UNEXPECTED FATHER Kelly Jamison

True, Hannah Brewster had never *told* Jordan McClennon that he was the father of the child she was looking after. But he was busy planning the perfect wedding when Hannah discovered what he suspected—and told him the truth!

### A MARRIAGE MADE IN JOEVILLE Anne Eames

*Montana Malones*

Savannah Smith had changed a great deal since her school days, but she'd never forgotten Ryder Malone. So she decided to go to Joeville to find out if the sexy loner was ready for marriage—and to go in disguise...

# COMING NEXT MONTH FROM

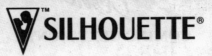 **SILHOUETTE**®

## Sensation

*A thrilling mix of passion, adventure
and drama*

**SERENA McKEE'S BACK IN TOWN** Marie Ferrarella
**SAVING SUSANNAH** Beverly Bird
**HIDE IN PLAIN SIGHT** Sara Orwig
**THE MAN SHE ALMOST MARRIED** Maggie Price

## Intrigue

*Danger, deception and desire*

**THE HERO'S SON** Amanda Stevens
**HER MOTHER'S ARMS** Kelsey Roberts
**AFTER THE DARK** Patricia Rosemoor
**WATCH OVER ME** Carly Bishop

## Special Edition

*Satisfying romances packed with emotion*

**THE NINE-MONTH MARRIAGE** Christine Rimmer
**THE RANCHER MEETS HIS MATCH** Patricia McLinn
**WILDCATTER'S KID** Penny Richards
**TEXAN'S BRIDE** Gail Link
**THE MAVERICK MARRIAGE** Cathy Gillen Thacker
**BABY ON HIS DOORSTEP** Diana Whitney

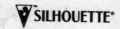

There must be something in the water in the little town of New Hope, there are certainly a lot of babies on the way! In this exciting new series, meet five delighted Mums-to-be.

And the handsome hunks who get some surprising news...

*Starting next month with:*

**THE BABY NOTION**
Dixie Browning
DESIRE October 1998

*Followed by:*

**BABY IN A BASKET**
Helen R. Myers
DESIRE November 1998

**MARRIED...WITH TWINS!**
Jennifer Mikels
SPECIAL EDITION December 1998

**HOW TO HOOK A HUSBAND (AND A BABY)**
Carolyn Zane
DESIRE January 1999

**DISCOVERED: DADDY**
Marilyn Pappano
SENSATION February 1999

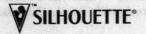

# JASMINE CRESSWELL

# THE DAUGHTER

Maggie Slade's been on the run for seven years now.
Seven years of living without a life or a future because
she's a woman with a past. And then she meets Sean
McLeod. Maggie has two choices. She can either run,
or learn to trust again and prove her innocence.

*"Romantic suspense at its finest."*

—Affaire de Coeur

1-55166-425-9
**AVAILABLE IN PAPERBACK
FROM SEPTEMBER, 1998**

# CHRISTIANE
# HEGGAN

# SUSPICION

Kate Logan's gut instincts told her that neither of her
clients was guilty of murder, and homicide detective
Mitch Calhoon wanted to help her prove it. What neither suspected was how dangerous the truth would be.

*"Christiane Heggan delivers a tale that will leave you
breathless."*

—Literary Times

**MIRA**®

**1-55166-305-8**
**AVAILABLE IN PAPERBACK**
**FROM SEPTEMBER, 1998**

# FIND THE FRUIT!

How would you like to win a year's supply of Silhouette® Books—FREE! Well, if you know your fruit, then you're already one step ahead when it comes to completing this competition, because all the answers are fruit! Simply decipher the code to find the names of ten fruit, complete the coupon overleaf and send it to us by 31st March 1999. The first five correct entries will each win a year's subscription to the Silhouette series of their choice. What could be easier?

| A | B | C | D | E | F | G | H | I |
|---|---|---|---|---|---|---|---|---|
| 15 |   |   |   |   | 20 |   |   |   |
| **J** | **K** | **L** | **M** | **N** | **O** | **P** | **Q** | **R** |
|   | 25 |   |   |   |   |   | 5 |   |
| **S** | **T** | **U** | **V** | **W** | **X** | **Y** | **Z** |   |
|   |   |   | 10 |   |   |   |   |   |

| 4 | 19 | 15 | 17 | 22 |
|---|----|----|----|----|
|   |    |    |    |    |

| 15 | 10 | 3 | 17 | 15 | 18 | 3 |
|----|----|---|----|----|----|---|
|    |    |   |    |    |    |   |

| 2 | 19 | 17 | 8 | 15 | 6 | 23 | 2 | 19 |
|---|----|----|---|----|---|----|---|----|
|   |    |    |   |    |   |    |   |    |

| 4 | 19 | 15 | 6 |
|---|----|----|---|
|   |    |    |   |

| 4 | 26 | 9 | 1 |
|---|----|---|---|
|   |    |   |   |

| 7 | 8 | 6 | 15 | 11 | 16 | 19 | 6 | 6 | 13 |
|---|---|---|----|----|----|----|---|---|----|
|   |   |   |    |    |    |    |   |   |    |

| 3 | 6 | 15 | 2 | 21 | 19 |
|---|---|----|---|----|----|
|   |   |    |   |    |    |

| 15 | 4 | 4 | 26 | 19 |
|----|---|---|----|----|
|    |   |   |    |    |

| 1 | 15 | 2 | 21 | 3 |
|---|----|---|----|---|
|   |    |   |    |   |

| 16 | 15 | 2 | 15 | 2 | 15 |
|----|----|---|----|---|----|
|    |    |   |    |   |    |

C8I

**Please turn over for details of how to enter →**

# HOW TO ENTER

There are ten coded words listed overleaf, which when decoded each spell the name of a fruit. There is also a grid which contains each letter of the alphabet and a number has been provided under some of the letters. All you have to do, is complete the grid, by working out which number corresponds with each letter of the alphabet. When you have done this, you will be able to decipher the coded words to discover the names of the ten fruit! As you decipher each code, write the name of the fruit in the space provided, then fill in the coupon below, pop this page into an envelope and post it today. Don't forget you could win a year's supply of Silhouette® Books—you don't even need to pay for a stamp!

Silhouette Find the Fruit Competition
FREEPOST CN81, Croydon, Surrey, CR9 3WZ
EIRE readers: (please affix stamp) PO Box 4546, Dublin 24.

Please tick the series you would like to receive if you
are one of the lucky winners

Desire™ ❏    Special Edition™ ❏    Sensation™ ❏    Intrigue™ ❏

Are you a Reader Service™ subscriber?          Yes ❏      No ❏

Ms/Mrs/Miss/Mr ................Initials .............................
                                          (BLOCK CAPITALS PLEASE)
Surname................................................................

Address ................................................................

...............................................................................

.............................................Postcode.........................

(I am over 18 years of age)                                    C8I

Closing date for entries is 31st March 1999. One entry per household.
Competition open to residents of the UK and Ireland only. As a result of this
application, you may receive further offers from Harlequin Mills &
Boon and other carefully selected companies. If you would prefer
not to share in this opportunity please write to The Data Manager,
P.O. Box 236, Croydon, Surrey CR9 3RU.
Silhouette is a registered trademark used under license.